A Long Farewell

COMMENTARY

"I really enjoy fiction that features our everyday efforts and struggles, especially in the world of work. *A Long Farewell* offers that snappy dialogue and reflective protagonist who inspires readers toward personal associations. The slice-of-life concept driving John Hagan's collection reminds us to slow down and contemplate what I've often called 'the complexity of simplicity.'"

—*Sherry Cook Stanforth, Ph.D.*
Director, Creative Writing Vision Program

"Every educator will laugh, cry, and understand; be perplexed by and relate to *A Long Farewell*. It touched me to my very core. [...] I think it was because of my love for and commitment to education. John Hagan captures the very heart of educators for whom those wonderful break-through moments [evoke] the tears and fears we have all experienced. I pulled *A Long Farewell* from the shelf and read the last few pages again. I did not want to put the book down [...] because I know...."

—*C. Daniel Raisch, Ph.D.*
Associate Dean, Education and Allied Professions
The University of Dayton

"John Hagan has a gift for short story telling. In *A Long Farewell* he offers us a collection of tales as varied as a college love and a Civil War specter. He paints very clear pictures of unusual situations with characters we can relate to. Using careful word choices, he makes his stories fit the genre without sacrificing the descriptions needed to be fascinating. I am a fan of this type of story, and John Hagan gives us a good dose."

—*Robert T. Sharp, D.V.M.*
Author
No Dogs in Heaven? Scenes from the Life of a Country Veterinarian

"[*A Long Farewell* is] reminiscent of my own childhood experiences growing up in Ohio. [...] The last story caught me completely by surprise, and I simply couldn't put the book down until I finished it. The book has mystery, intrigue, and humor. Thanks, John Hagan, for easy and relaxing hours."

—*Kathleen Manor*
Reader
Grosse Pointe Woods, Michigan

"John Hagan's *A Long Farewell* is an excellent short-story collection that moves seamlessly between his realistic use of Ohio diction to passages from Shakespeare, Tennyson, Hawthorne, and other classical writers, an obvious fusion of his experiences in Southern Ohio and his English teaching profession. While many of the stories are drawn from Hagan's educational background, there is something for everyone in *A Long Farewell*, and everyone can find something of him or herself in the book. Whether you read the book from front-to-back or choose the order of the stories does not matter. What does matter is that you read this book."

—*Caitlin M. Ryan*
Associate Editor
The Highland County Press

"John Hagan's short stories range across the experiences of a seven-year-old boy, high school/college student, teacher/principal, and retiree. He captures nostalgic scenes of yesteryear in remarkable detail and with subtle charm. His love for the English language, world literature, Quarter Horses, and local color reflects his sensitivity for the environment and human nature, and it affects his story-telling style. *A Long Farewell* is more than the creation of educator characters and realistic surprises. It is an intriguing read in which to delight."

—*Carolyn M. Gravelle, Ph.D.*
Consultant
Pine Orchard, Inc.

"John Hagan has a knack for telling a story with such a passion and an attention to detail that the reader cannot help but be drawn into the story, as if it were a shared experience. His vivid descriptions and his remarkable ability to depict the people and places in his stories give readers a feeling of déjà vu, as if they were there while each story unfolds. *A Long Farewell's* emphasis on realism and ease of reading moves readers through each story, while it evokes smiles and head nodding among those from every background or walk of life. Thoroughly enjoyed and heartily recommended."

—*David S. Vail, Ph.D.*
Superintendent
Miamisburg City Schools

A Long Farewell

John Hagan

Goose River Press
Waldoboro, Maine

PUBLISHER'S NOTE

A Long Farewell is a collection of short stories. Exclusive of historical figures, other nationally prominent individuals, and documented events or factual locations; the names, characters, places, and incidents portrayed herein are fictitious. Any similarity to actual persons (living or deceased), events, or locations is coincidental or inferred.

Library of Congress Control Card Number: 2009927931

ISBN: 978-1-59715-081-3

Tenth Printing, 2017

Front Cover Photo by John Hagan
Back Cover Photo by Joseph Gural

Published by
Goose River Press
3400 Friendship Road
Waldoboro, Maine 05472
www.gooseriverpress.com

Dedication

*To the teachers who guide the nation's youth
toward proficiency in a broad range of curricula
and who imbue their pupils with a love of learning,
a reverence for truth,
and a belief in the family of humanity.*

Contents

Also by John Hagan

An Irish View of the Country

Ties That Inspire

"Bucolic Images"
(*Goose River Anthology, 2014*)

"An Old Friend Called"
(*Goose River Anthology, 2012*)

"Saddle Pals"
(*Goose River Anthology, 2010*)

"Churchyard"
(*Goose River Anthology, 2008*)

For

"Flash"

and

"Barracuda"

And therefore every gentil wight I preye,

...

Whoso list it nat yheere,

Turne over the leef and chese another tale;

...

Blameth nat me if that ye chese amys.

The Canterbury Tales
Geoffrey Chaucer

Let Me Play the Fool

Let me play the fool,
With mirth and laughter let old wrinkles come,
And let my liver rather heat with wine
Than my heart cool with mortifying groans.
—The Merchant of Venice
William Shakespeare

McGinnis died last week. He dropped dead running up a hill he'd run at least a hundred times. He must have had some little monster in one of the vessels of his heart that all that high school football, weeknight softball, and late-night draught beer wouldn't awaken, but sensible and regular exercise caused to rear its ugly head. From all accounts, his routine was very much like the four- or five-mile route Quinn ran three or four times per week, trying to red herring the Grim Reaper as much as possible.

The cars were parked almost bumper-to-bumper now as Kevin Quinn eased his own down the decaying, dreary street. His thoughts began to ramble in a stream of consciousness that shifted its course with virtually every house he passed. The old neighborhood—he'd spent the first twenty-three years of his life in the white two-story he was now approaching, and he paused to reflect in a kind of ambivalence as a wave of bittersweet memories flooded his mind. Things were so different now. Besides the departure of all the families he'd known so well, the street was showing signs of steady decline. His own house was symptomatic of the entire neighborhood: tawdry curtains hanging akimbo in dirty windows, exterior paint chipping out of control, and unsightly foxtail and crabgrass vying for possession of a depressing yard.

This house was most closely associated with the word "home" for him and his two brothers. He'd give anything for a look inside again; he knew every inch of it.

He drove under the electric wires that stretched from utility pole to utility pole across the street and had loomed as a rite of passage for any kid who dared to join in the neighborhood touch football games played in the street between the curbs. Typically, the games began as two-handed touch, but arguments as to whether both hands had touched fabric or flesh invariably erupted, so a well-placed bash in the ball carrier's back, which sent him sprawling to the pavement, was a no-brainer regarding the two-hand contact requirement and resulted in abrasions on hands, elbows, and knees that were worn like red badges of courage. The test of your skill as a quarterback was in completing a forward pass by throwing the ball over the electric wires with enough precision to hit your receiver in a fly pattern to the end zone, marked by an imaginary line running from the rear bumper of a white Chevy hardtop to the curb on the opposite side of the street. Somehow, the power lines didn't seem nearly as high now, nor did the street seem nearly wide enough for those games of legend.

Quinn had been a high school teacher most of his adult life as he made his way down the street past the home of his youth. He made this trip quite impulsively but not frequently. The house was the base of operations for so many of the experiences of his childhood that were more vivid in his recollection than those that he had had just a day or two before. Damned if he couldn't just about hear his mom yelling for him out the front screen door again like so many times on those summer nights when the rest of the kids were on home base in a game of kick-the-can, and he and Tina Castianno crouched together in one of the window wells of old Mrs. Kelly's huge home.

Tina was a raven-haired, brown-eyed Italian kid who had made him aware of the pleasing differences between boys and girls before they were twelve. She would whisper to him in the darkness, "Wait a few more minutes," before they broke with cat-like speed for the old soup can. Her directive was all it would take to keep him hunkered down by the basement window. The sweat glistening on her forehead, her thick black hair curled by the heat, and the deep but casually acquired tan on those satiny legs and arms that filled the openings of her home-cut short shorts and sleeveless T-shirts were already distracting his attention from the time-honored rituals of games like kick-the-can, gang tag, and flashlight tag. Tina was the only kid his age in the neighborhood who could outrun him, and her status as fastest-on-the-street earned her Kevin's unspoken admiration in addition to his emerging prurient interests. Her imaginative strengths were never more manifest than when she and Kevin roller-skated together in the parking lot of the nearby E.U.B. Church. Pitted against mortal enemies in their version of a roller-derby battle to the death, Tina would conjure evil incarnate adversaries like Cobra Fang Woman, Bear Claw Boy, and Scorpion Tail Man. She would eventually move to Colorado with her family and leave Kevin forever wondering what the adult manifestation of that Atalanta with the sinewy body and creative mind became.

As a kid and through some of his adulthood, Kevin had two really close friends, Matt McGinnis and Brian Doyle. He also had three heroes who claimed his inveterate loyalty in stages and remained demigods in his mind long after experience, maturity, and age should have put their deeds in perspective: Roy Rogers, Mickey Mantle, and Pete Dawkins.

Matt, Brian, and Kevin became aware of themselves in the fifties, even though sociologists would probably call them products of the sixties, finishing high school and college as they did in that turbulent decade of change and unrest. He had other school buddies, of course: Willy Brennan, Sean McCarthy, Bobby Malone, and Lannie Bohanan, to name a few; some of them rich, some of them not so rich, most of them Irish, and all of them Catholic. Some were sons of doctors; some were sons of company owners; some were sons of laborers, but most were just little sonsabitches. They were, however, all products of the very Irish Saint Joseph's Parish and School, and their parents all dutifully sent them to Saint Aloysius High School, the all-male institution that was sequel to their collective indoctrination into Catholic dogma.

Kevin's brothers were significantly older than he; one of whom was a rowdy, party animal and the envy of all of Kevin's buddies, and the other was the quintessential Jack Armstrong, All-American-Boy type, who played football for West Point and was the dotage of his father. Given the times and his family dynamics, it was easy for Kevin to embrace with unbridled fanaticism Rogers, Mantle, and Dawkins as his personal champions, who were, at various stages of his development, his *raison d'etre*: he was on Earth to pay homage to these luminaries.

Roy Rogers didn't belong to him alone, of course; he knew that; he just didn't believe that. They rode together on the black fence that separated his back yard from an alley that ran behind his garage. It was an odd-looking iron fence with a six-inch flat top that allowed him to sling some throw rugs over for a saddle and on which to park his skinny little butt. With a piece of rope strung around the flat top and serving as the reins for his trusty steed and with his feet hooked into the crisscrossed stays that made for nifty stirrups, he rode the range with Roy, and together they kicked butt and took names. A Saturday matinee at the Dayview Theater with Roy starring in *My Pal Trigger, Grand Canyon Trail, Home in Oklahoma,* or *Down Dakota Way* provided enough grist for his imaginative mill to keep him in backyard episodes for a month. Nothing was more appealing to him than when Roy played a kind of maverick or pariah who had to prove his probity in the face of suspicion and adversity before he restored his honor and won the girl. Kevin had a few Gene Autry T-shirts with iron-on images, a pair of Hopalong

A Long Farewell

Cassidy six-guns with *bas-relief* handles, and a Lone Ranger silver bullet with a compass inside, but hell, Roy Rogers was the King of the Cowboys. A boy couldn't do better than Roy.

Roy was pretty much the controlling influence of Kevin's single-digit years, during which he languished in a world of daydreams and other flights of fancy. School was rapidly becoming the bane of his existence and would remain so throughout his formal education. This developing distaste for the demands of scholarship was traceable in part to the daily drone of black-garbed, bead-rattling nuns who made every effort to convince him that his body was a temple of the devil and his thoughts were grievously inappropriate. The fact that his family was among the poorer ones whose snot-nosed kids roamed the halls of Saint Joseph's in hand-me-down corduroy pants, which made them sound like they were farting with every step, contributed to making him an eight-year *persona non grata*. The nuns typically regarded doctors' and executives' children as the *crème de la crème* of the school. With few exceptions girls were held in high regard, but only those who if they died suddenly would bolt directly into Heaven took their turns as the reigning Queens-of-the-May.

An exception to the nuns' preference for the distaff side of the school family was Sandra Blakely, who showed up for seventh grade sporting a firm and ample pair of breasts and found sundry and creative ways of bumping them into the bashful boys whose days were made by a serendipitous encounter with THE BABE's boobs. Sandra met her wanton Waterloo one late-spring day in the eighth grade, however, when she rendezvoused with Lannie Bohanan in the wrap room during the noon hour, a time when the rest of the boy dolts were out on the playground playing keep-away with a football. Bohanan had "been around the block" a time or two, having spent some quality time with Protestant and Jewish girls who'd let you have a quick feel if you played your cards right. The wrap room was the narrow, hall-like area at the rear of each classroom with a row of hooks on each wall for wool coats and knit hats in the winter and windbreakers and baseball hats in the spring. The seventh and eighth grade wrap-room hooks also accommodated the traffic boys' badge belts, sign poles, and rain slickers.

Sister Roberta Anne, principal and one of the eighth grade teachers, didn't keep her appointed rounds in the cafeteria, restrooms, and alcoves on Sandra's fateful day; rather, she returned to her classroom surreptitiously during the noon hour for some inexplicable reason and found Sandra tucked in between the rain slickers with her boobs out, her panties down, and Bohanan's hands up her jumper, groping her fine, firm buns. What lasting impact this vicarious participation in carnal pleasure had upon the good sister's psyche remains one of the mysteries of the Catholic Church, but some facts are known. Roberta Anne rousted the two sinners from the devil's clutches, and while marching them to her office, she excoriated them for their brazen affront to her chastity. By 1:30, however, she had regained her composure enough to assign the rest of her students an in-class essay on the merits of one of the beatitudes: blessed are the pure of heart. After a contrite appearance before the dour and saintly Monsignor Murphy, Bohanan sustained only a brief suspension, which ended in time for the traffic boys' spring trip to the Cincinnati Reds game, but Sandra didn't return to Saint Joseph's for the remaining classes, the group picture, or the graduation Mass. Bohanan, however, regaled all the guys with his lurid account of the scandalous ordeal on the bus ride to and from Cincinnati. A lingering suspicion long after college years among the boys was that Sandra's tragic flaw was her need for adulation, and thus her sharing of her forthcoming tryst with a trusted classmate, who conventional wisdom suggested was Queen-of-the-May Rosetherese Reilly, resulted in her unceremonious and immediate removal from staid old Saint Joseph's. The reason for Roberta Anne's departure that day from her ritualistic rounds and her atypical return to the classroom could only be conjectured. Hester Prynne cut a better deal than Sandra Blakely.

One of the factors that made the precepts of Papal pontifications bearable for Kevin was in the person of a freckle-faced, soft-bodied, sandy-haired miscreant known as "Dirty Doyle," or Brian Doyle to those who failed to recognize the devious mind that roiled behind his cherubic face. Kevin and Brian discovered their potential for misadventure when Kevin's mother invited Brian to Kevin's eighth birthday party because she believed he came from really fine people. Sensing their mutual penchant for wickedness before either expressed it, Kevin and Brian bolted the party early and left the rest of the invitees to the inanities of Pin the Tail on the Donkey and other traditional party games while they entertained themselves with a fifty-cent balsa airplane down at Kelly's Field. They climbed trees, hatched plans, and returned home well after dark to their nearly apoplectic mothers who were on the brink of asking the local constabulary to drag the river. Thus began a forged friendship that would end only when world developments intruded upon their lives and left them separated forever.

Quinn turned the corner and headed down the alley to the now-abandoned building that once housed Myrtle's Delicatessen, the mythical birthplace of a fellow named Mickey Mantle.

Mickey Mantle was, in Kevin's mind at least, his discovery by reason of his finding the slugger on a baseball card one day while walking home from Myrtle's with some of the guys in his neighborhood who cheered the Cincinnati Reds because of their close location. Myrtle was the three-hundred-pound behemoth who dispensed ice cream from the corner of a right triangle-shaped delicatessen and whose Mary Jane's, Bazooka Gum, Tootsie Rolls, and every other tooth decaying edible attracted the neighborhood street runners like ants to a jellyroll. For Myrtle, a hand-dipped cone for the customer-kid meant one scoop for him for every two scoops for her, deposited directly into her prodigious jowls. Myrtle's sanitation system consisted of her plunging the scooper periodically into a murky vat of tepid water that she changed with religious fervor, twice weekly. Seemingly wedged in perpetuity at the merger of the two walls forming the most acute angle of the store, Myrtle barked directives, took nickels and dimes, and reigned regally over this enchanting place where gourmet dining was as available as a quick strike on your old lady's purse.

Kevin opened his Topps bubblegum-baseball cards after one of these idyllic visits and found this young outfielder for the New York Yankees whose alliterative name appealed to him more than any career statistics. Although Mantle was a virtual unknown in Cincinnati Reds country, he made rapid advances in Kevin's personal heroes' corner. With every monster blast off the bat and every sensational catch of the ball that Kevin read about in the local newspaper, The Mick became less of a man and more of a deity. Kevin rarely got to see his hero on television, and, as such, no human foibles or character flaws sullied his perceptions of Mantle. He was pretty damned sure that Simon Peter sat on the right hand of Mickey Mantle.

One of the first sterling qualities he discovered about Matt McGinnis was in his declaration that Mickey Mantle was also his favorite baseball player, but Kevin held a private resentment that Matt was a Johnny-come-lately to the local Mickey Mantle fan club and a bit of a usurper to his self-anointed presidency of this august organization.

Quinn drove on and headed toward the old parish neighborhood of Saint Joseph's, eventually finding himself moving slowly past Matt McGinnis's family home. As close as Kevin was to Matt and Brian, Matt and Brian were not of a kindred spirit; they were friendly but not close. Kevin and Brian were bonded by imagination, creativity, and mischief; Kevin and Matt were bonded by athletics, heroes, and mischief.

A Long Farewell

From his earliest recollections of Matt, Kevin had always been in awe of and in competition with his friend on what General Douglas MacArthur had called "the fields of friendly strife." On the playground and later in Catholic Youth Organization sports, Matt invariably excelled. He was blessed with the perfectly proportioned body for each level of competition. In C.Y.O., which even casual observers knew really stood for Crucify Your Opponent, Matt would always be just below the football upper-weight limit without a pound of fat on him. He and Kevin played C.Y.O. football, basketball, and baseball together, but Matt was always the star, and Kevin was always one of the underweight and undersized support players whose role was to situate Matt for the touchdown, jump shot, or run-batted-in.

At huge Saint Aloysius High School the competition to make one of the Knights' big three sports was fierce. Owing to his height, Kevin never figured to make the basketball team, and largely because he couldn't hit his weight, baseball was never his particular favorite, but football was his passion. His oldest and much bigger brother had been a scholar-athlete at Saint Aloysius and had made the all-area teams in football and baseball, going on to play football for some of Army's most powerful teams in the fifties.

This family connection with West Point gave rise to Kevin's fascination with Army's Heisman Award winning Pete Dawkins, whose status at the Academy as an All-American football player, All-East hockey player, first captain of the Corps of Cadets, star man (top 5% of his class), senior class president, and Rhodes Scholar made him the exemplar of everything that Kevin dreamed of but physical and intellectual limitations would never allow him to achieve. This interest in Dawkins, the Renaissance Man, would only be reinforced for Kevin over many years, as the Army star went on to earn an M.A. at Oxford University; win two Bronze Stars for valor and the Vietnamese Cross for gallantry; earn a Ph.D. at Princeton; become one of the nation's youngest brigadier generals; and play a wicked trumpet, piano, guitar, and trombone.

Kevin, by contrast, was barely able to make the Saint Aloysius football team in his junior year after two previous attempts ended with his name's being posted ignominiously on the cut sheet tacked on the bulletin board outside the shower room. In the meantime Matt had not only made the squad each year but was a high-profile player on a team that was a perennial state power. In their senior year, Kevin, now at a husky 5'10" and 155 pounds, gained enough playing time to earn a varsity letter because he was finally able to turn coaches' heads with sheer speed, but Matt, at 6' and 189 pounds, made all-area as a running back and plugged in at strong safety when the Knights were backed up to their goal line. For some reason, Kevin always felt more secure and confident at cornerback when Matt came into the game on defense. This feeling characterized his whole relationship with Matt, even though he would chide Kevin unmercifully during the games, and for years later in bars and at parties, he would laugh raucously while he embellished Kevin's blunders on the field and in the classroom.

Quinn rounded the corner and headed down the hill toward Saint Joseph's School and Parish. Saint Joe's was the hot house that had provided the fertile soil and climate for the development of life-long friendships for so many of its pupils. Here, of course, Kevin and Brian had formulated many of their nefarious plots. One, perpetrated in the eighth grade, ran them afoul of Mr. Orville Thompson when they were desperate to meet the traffic boys' merit-point minimum for making the annual odyssey to the Cincinnati Reds game. Since they were both in arrears in their contributions to the stop-sign pole collection drive, they decided there was scant time to round up handles from household brooms and mops from their mothers and neighbors. Stop-sign poles were those that were used to hold the American Automobile Association-sponsored STOP flags for traffic boys to alert approaching drivers to the squirrelly kids who were about to cross the street individually or *en masse*.

Based upon Brian's compelling impetus, "I've got a great idea," he and Kevin broke into Orville's equipment closet, borrowed one of his handsaws, and purloined his entire ensemble of mops and brooms during their lunch break. Locating themselves in one of the stairwells, they began their eleventh-hour quest for the merit points by sawing the handles from the business ends of Orville's cherished equipment. Murphy's Law brought Orville around the corner and into the stairwell just as Brian had severed the handle from the last mop.

The cataclysm that ensued stood for many years as one of the defining incidents in Saint Joseph's storied history. Thompson, with a shirt collar in each hand, dragged the ashen poachers up to Roberta Anne's office, screaming uncontrollably while saliva dripped down his chin from a bloated cheek of Mail Pouch he chewed each day to calm his nerves. Summoned immediately by Roberta Anne was Sister Loretta Margaret because she was in charge of the traffic boys and had instituted the stop-sign pole collection drive. Loretta Margaret was also the endearing and fun-loving young nun who spent an hour after school one snowy day judging the boys' wipeouts as they raced down the steep playground hill on an eight-foot, two-by-twelve pine board they affectionately and reverently addressed as Big Beulah.

Kevin and Brian knew that Loretta Margaret was their buddy and that she had defended them in many a difficult scrape, but this caper might just exceed the limits of her intervention. After a full minute of Thompson's screaming at record-setting decibels, Roberta Anne directed the custodian to describe what had happened for Loretta Margaret's edification. Loretta Margaret's theatrical scowl toward the cowering scoundrels notwithstanding, Kevin thought he detected a gleam in her eye that betrayed a twisted admiration for his and Brian's novel approach to pole procurement. After all, she needed those damned handles as much as Thompson. Roberta Anne, however, was not pleased, and she handed down the death penalty: no Cincinnati Reds trip for these incorrigible curs. About a day before the big trip, however, Roberta Anne rescinded her decree, and she allowed Kevin and Brian to join the others, largely because leaving them behind posed a serious threat to the school, not to mention Orville's sanity.

As Quinn passed the old school and approached the Spanish-style church, he was reminded of his and Doyle's participation in the most memorable solemn high Mass ever celebrated in Saint Joseph's Parish. Nothing prior or subsequent to it ever equaled its sheer drama and excitement. Principal among the players in this melodrama was the young and high-strung assistant pastor Father Terence O'Donnell. In addition to the good priest was an entourage of altar boys that included the pedantic and authoritative college sophomore Ralph Bergdoll as the master of ceremonies, Kevin's rascal brother Danny and his best buddy Sean McCormick, and, among others, Kevin and Brian. Kevin and Brian were the only high school freshmen, and three or four, including Kevin's brother, were home for the holidays from college.

While they donned their cassocks and surplices, Kevin and Brian were lectured by Bergdoll in his most unctuous terms about the solemnity of the Mass and the lofty expectations that Father O'Donnell had regarding acolyte decorum. In his less sanctified words, Bergdoll didn't want any "screw-ups from two little farts who could make me look like shit as the master of ceremonies."

The Mass, celebrating the Feast of the Circumcision, began peacefully enough at twelve o'clock on New Year's Day. Kevin and Brian had few responsibilities, but one was to stand to the right of the altar and on Bergdoll's cues pick up the candles situated on knee-high, ornamental holders and move to prominent locations around the sanctuary. While

A Long Farewell

Kevin and Brian took their positions at the back of the sanctuary and to the right of the altar, Kevin's brother and McCormick were cavorting in the acolytes' sacristy and attempting to prepare the incensor for later use in the Mass. Waiting for his and Brian's first order from Bergdoll to move to a directed spot in the sanctuary, Kevin noticed about twenty, three-foot decorative candleholders with partially consumed candles that ran side-by-side for about ten yards behind the altar. Each of the wooden holders was equipped near the top with a glass, wax catcher that encircled the base of the candle. The candles and holders had obviously been used to enhance the beauty of the sanctuary during the Christmas Masses and were now awaiting the sacristan's relocation of them to a more permanent storage area.

By about three quarters of the way through the Mass or at about the hour-and-a-half mark, Kevin and Brian had made two or three trips around the altar and dutifully returned to their low-profile positions at the rear of the sanctuary. Only Brian's momentary loss of balance resulting from a trip on his own cassock when moving the ponderous liturgy book from the gospel to epistle side of the altar had slightly marred the dignity of the ceremony. At this point, Kevin, with hands together and fingers pointing to Heaven, began to doze a bit. He was brought to perfect alertness, however, when he observed parishioners rushing up the aisles toward the sanctuary in a panic-stricken state. In the next instant, two of the older acolytes were beating him about the arm, shoulder, and chest while pandemonium reigned throughout the church. The billowy sleeve of Kevin's heavily starched white surplice had caught fire in the candleholder he had set next to himself on the floor of the sanctuary. To his total astonishment, he had been engulfed in flames, and in an instant he was more radiant than the gold-plated monstrance.

After the commotion subsided and the shaken worshipers returned to their pews, Kevin went to the sacristy to replace his surplice, only to find his brother and McCormick convulsed with laughter and abusing him mercilessly. Before Kevin could rejoin Brian for the last segment of the Mass, Bergdoll re-entered the sacristy and began to flay him with the sharpest kind of language. Since Bergdoll was an inch or two shorter than Kevin, the image of the agitated master of ceremonies gesticulating upward into the face of the terrified offender sent another shockwave of laughter through Danny and McCormick. Bergdoll marched out of the sacristy and back to the sanctuary, followed in lockstep by Kevin.

The *coup de grâce* was delivered to Father O'Donnell's solemn high Mass when he turned to the congregation to bestow his final blessing upon the faithful. Eager to show his contempt for Kevin and Brian, Bergdoll had pushed in beside them to await the besieged priest's last words. In so doing, Bergdoll's elbow bumped the end candleholder that Kevin had observed earlier in the Mass. In his vain attempt to arrest its fall, Bergdoll only increased the velocity of the candle's descent, and it struck the next candle, commencing a domino effect that produced a staccato of wax catchers smashing to the hardwood floor behind the altar and ending with a crescendo that shot countless chunks of broken glass clear to the archway of the priest's sacristy, giving a cruet-spilling start to the preoccupied Monsignor Murphy, who had slipped in the back door for a quick nip from his private stock of Mass wine.

No one was completely sure whether Father O'Donnell actually delivered his final blessing, but some behaviors were specifically noted. Danny and McCormick had been reduced to maniacal laughter; Bergdoll was in a crimson fury; the congregation was spellbound with one or two devout souls seeming to speak in tongues, and Brian had actually peed his pants a little.

When Kevin and Brian entered the priest's sacristy to assist the dignified man-of-the-cloth with the storage of his vestments, they found him arched forward with his head down and his hands on the edge of the Formica top that ran the length of the storage drawers. When Brian said in his most obsequious tone, "Father, may I take your chasuble?" the stupefied priest turned slowly and gave him and Kevin a look that transformed his angelic face into a sinister aspect and wordlessly declared that their services were no longer required. As they left the priest's sacristy, Kevin was sure that he heard graphic expletives escape the lips of a man of God.

As Quinn drove home, he concluded that McGinnis and Doyle were to friendship what Xerox was to copying and Kleenex was to tissue. Their Celtic surnames were as synonymous to cronies as certain brand names were to commodities. Quinn had lost Doyle during the Tet Offensive when a Vietcong mortar round hit the quarters where the lieutenant was sleeping and killed him instantly.

A Frankenstein Night

The whole neighborhood abounds with local tales,
Haunted spots, and twilight superstitions; [...]
And the nightmare [...] seems to make it
The favorite scene of her gambols.
—The Legend of Sleepy Hollow
Washington Irving

Walking across a railroad trestle under a harvest moon at 10:45 was an adventure that seven-year-old Matty McGuire wished he had considered more carefully about a half-hour earlier when his two older brothers and three older cousins were making their clandestine break from the old farmhouse to the drive-in theater down the road. Earlier that day he had eavesdropped on the five of them as they made plans in the saddle room to sneak out the window from a second-floor bedroom on to the bay window and down the adjacent trellis to watch one of the last movies of the season at the Stardust Drive-in Theater. They had already tried to "ditch" Matty in the morning, but he knew from experience that their high-level caucuses were always held in the lean-to of the hay barn where his Uncle Joe kept the saddles and other tack for Dawn and Glory, the two Morgan horses that were as integral to Kerrigan family life as the three Border Collies were that shadowed the boys around the farm all day and slept in the spacious kitchen of the cavernous house all night. When the five older boys tried to make their escape around 10:15, Matty threatened to expose them if they didn't take him along. It was a crisp but comfortable Saturday night in mid October, and Matty and his two brothers, Sean and Danny, had arrived Friday afternoon for another delightful sojourn at their Aunt Katy and Uncle Joe's sylvan paradise that would

16

all too soon be consumed by urban sprawl.

Matty's Aunt Kathleen, or Aunt Katy as she was affectionately called, was one of his dad's seven siblings, and she had married the Irish farm boy Joe Kerrigan about three years before the bombing of Pearl Harbor. Aiden McGuire, Matty's dad, and Joe were both World War II veterans. Aiden, a captain in the Army Air Corps, had served as a ground support officer at B-17 bases, and Joe, a land-lover who had joined the Navy after the Japanese attack, had risen to petty officer first class by the war's end. A rangy 6'3" before enlistment, Joe's return to farm work had increased his musculature, but his frequent beer consumption had ballooned his girth. Many a summer evening would find him storming into the kitchen from the fields, popping the caps from two Blatz beers on a Coca-Cola bottle opener, and draining both brews in an eye-popping display of beer-chugging prowess.

As a seven-year-old, Matty was six years his brother Sean's junior and four years his brother Danny's. His cousins Colin, Tommy, and Patty were twelve, eleven, and ten-years-old respectively, and they were three of Aunt Katy and Uncle Joe's four sons. Franky, the youngest, was only two, and each day he challenged the spindled sides of his playpen in the dooryard or kitchen, wearing a pee-soaked diaper in near perpetuity. While not the oldest of the group, Tommy at eleven was, nevertheless, the inspirational leader of every venture into the forbidden zones, which included the gravel pit's lake, the Hereford bull's pasture, the house's widow walk, the grain silo's ladder, and the B&O Railroad's trestle. Tommy had not only tested and mastered them all, but he held the standing record for time spent (seventy-five seconds) in the field with Old Buster, the eighteen-hundred-pound mass of bovine muscle and semen that ruled his domain like an Egyptian pharaoh, serviced Uncle Joe's feeder cows with a religious zeal, and dispatched bipedal intruders with an alarming alacrity.

John Hagan

The boys had traversed a bean field, a wood lot, and a cornfield before they reached the tractor path that ran next to the Mad River and the trestle that crossed it. They could easily have taken the dirt and gravel road that ran past the farm lane to the state route and then to the theater about a mile farther down, but that would have required more travel time and would have brought them to the front gate of the drive-in, preventing easy access to the "complimentary" seating behind the chain-link fence, just beyond the last row of cars and speakers. The dirt and gravel road was ambiguously named Prince Albert Drive, after either the austere Queen Victoria's husband or the popular pipe tobacco. The boys' unmarried and urbane Aunt Margaret, whom all the cousins called Aunt Maggie in her absence, often took the Greyhound bus to visit her sister Kathleen after a taxing week in the city as a legal secretary. She invariably glowered at the crusty driver on that route when he rudely and flamboyantly announced the Prince Albert Drive stop as "Tobacco Road!" Much like the oft-vexed British queen, Aunt Maggie was not amused. Matty had once overheard one of his teenaged cousins say that Aunt Maggie reminded her of the spinster whom Oliver Wendell Holmes describes in his playful poem "My Aunt."

Once on the trestle, Tommy led the way, followed by Sean, Colin, Patty, Danny, and Matty. The trestle was roughly a hundred yards long and spanned a shallow stretch of the Mad River. It provided a forty to fifty-foot drop in the middle, and its crossties were gapped at about six to eight inches each. Whatever the spacing, Matty was convinced that one misstep would send him plunging through a gap to sudden death on the rocks or in the river below. In his excitement, however, he had taken about ten steps on to the trestle before his fears had taken control of his feet. By then, Tommy and the others, aided by the moonlight and plenty of practice, had bounded over the crossties out to about forty yards away. In spite of his daily irritations with his pesky little brother, Danny instinctively looked for Matty and saw him gripped in terror and staring down through the crossties.

"C'mon, ya little fart! What're ya waitin' for?"

"I'm gonna fall through these boards!"

"No, you're not. Just watch your step and be careful."

"It's so high up here. I'm really scared!"

Either because he remembered his own trepidations during his first crossing or just because Matty seemed so vulnerable, Danny went back and coached his brother across the trestle. In the meantime, the others had bunched up at Tommy, who was irritated by the delay.

"I knew he'd hold us up."

Sean, struck by Patty's display of brotherly concern, offered his measure of sibling defense. "Shut up. They're comin'."

By the time these juvenile fugitives reached the rolling field of red clover adjacent to the grounds of the drive-in, the feature movie, *Frankenstein,* was well in-progress, a necessary development they had to accept if they were to avoid the parental detection that might result from a premature escape attempt from the farmhouse. Since all but Matty had seen the film at least once previously in an indoor theater, no one was too disappointed by the late arrival. Typical of most drive-in theaters, the Stardust ran its coming attractions, short newsies, and color cartoons from 9:00 until about 10:30, so most of what the boys had missed was only the film's preamble to the fitful acts of the monster's savagery. Taking their seats in the clover, the five older boys buttoned up their coats and pulled up their collars. Matty mimicked their every move and feigned a blithe detachment as the Boris Karloff monster stampeded the clownish villagers and strangled his bug-eyed victims. Hours past his bedtime, Matty watched most of the movie fighting an oppressive drowsiness, but he knew that any request to leave would be met with merciless broadsides of "told-ya-so's" from the others.

As gathering clouds obscured the moon, the only ambient lighting emanated from the movie screen, and it flickered across the faces of the six escapees, causing a ghoulish result that rivaled the scariest scenes of the film. In the absence of speakers to provide diabolical dialogue, morose music, and eerie effects, the silence of the autumn night, pierced only by the esoteric discourse of two owls, made the black-and-white movie images seem all the more sinister. By the time the monster bellowed from the burning windmill at his pitchfork-wielding pursuers, Matty was so distressed by his gothic surroundings he wished he'd never heard of the Stardust Drive-in Theater.

"C'mon," said Colin to the others as the movie credits began to roll. "We've gotta get our butts movin'.'"

"Do we have to cross that trestle again?" asked the mournful Matty.

"Well, we can't just fly across the river, can we?" said Tommy, whose own fatigue and anxieties were beginning to take their toll.

What Matty couldn't know was that the daunting railroad trestle would be the least of his fears before he awakened in the morning to one of Aunt Katy's sumptuous Sunday breakfasts, the aromas from which wafted up from the kitchen and beckoned the boys like Homeric sirens.

Arriving at the trestle, Matty looked upon it with a dread reserved for the most detestable of man-made or natural hazards. Given the late hour and the absence of the benevolent moonlight, all the boys now regarded the trestle as a kind of wooden-toothed beast that lay before them like a dragon lurking in a hostile forest.

Sean, recognizing Matty's understandable fears, said to the others, "You guys go ahead; I'll walk with Matty."

The other four started across much more apprehensively and carefully than they had earlier, and Sean stayed just behind Matty with a hand firmly on his little brother's shoulder. Since the crossing took much more time than anticipated, an unspoken but almost palpable fear began to engulf the boys. The elapsed time since their departure from the house was beginning to mount beyond their expectations, and the cloaking darkness was enveloping them like an atmospheric gelatin. Once across the trestle, they followed the paths between the cornrows rather easily, and they quickened their pace and gained a little time.

The Kerrigan boys knew that the wood lot would be even more of a challenge than the trestle, but if they picked their way carefully and stayed together, they should find the bean field quickly and be pretty much home free. Making better progress than even Colin thought they would, the situation seemed favorable until Patty said to the group, "Did'ya hear that?"

"Hear what?" asked the impatient Danny.

Everyone tuned his ears to hear what he hoped Patty had imagined. For a good thirty seconds, the boys heard nothing but their own breathing.

"C'mon," stage-whispered Tommy.

As they started forward, a voice broke the silence about fifty yards to their left, and as it rose in decibels, it raised goose bumps on all their arms, legs, necks, and backs. It lasted at least eight seconds before it died completely. In lung-stopping terror, the boys tried to divine the voice's exact location and identity.

Once more it screamed, now clearly the voice of a woman in horrendous agony or inestimable fear.

"Aaaiiieee. Aaaiiieee."

"Oh, no!" said Tommy. "It's the woman who was buried alive that Joshua told us about. Keep goin' or she'll rip our throats out."

Joshua was the ne'er-do-well loafer from down the road on Prince Albert Drive, who worked just enough for Joe Kerrigan to support a thriving whiskey habit and buy fuel for a Warm Morning stove that chased the chill from a three-room shanty. The boys knew he was little or no help to their

21

father and that his pay was mostly a gift, but what he lacked in industry he replaced in folklore. He had once told the boys of a woman from the "farm over yonder" who, prior to the Civil War, had been buried alive by her husband, claiming she had died from the cholera. Everyone knew he was "meaner than a snake and crooked as a dog's hind leg," according to Joshua, so most folks in the vicinity just knew she wasn't dead when he buried her.

"Aaaiiieee. Aaaiiieee."

The cries now seemed almost next to the boys but remained baffling. Staying as close together as possible, the brothers and cousins navigated the remainder of the wood lot efficiently and set personal night-speed records for crossing the bean field. Tongue-paralyzing fear prevented even nervous chatter until they cleared the soybeans.

Only much later when the Kerrigan boys told their story of the alive-dead woman to their father did he tell them she was probably only a red fox that can sound almost like a woman in terror. Colin, Tommy, and Patty never shared that detail with their McGuire cousins.

Returning to the dooryard at 12:40, the boys were just about to begin their one-by-one climb up the trellis when the house lights came on and the kitchen door opened simultaneously. On to the small porch stepped Uncle Joe, whose natural insouciance and affability were often disguised by his imposing height, his bloated beer belly, and his ham-like forearms. Aunt Katy stood in the doorway, silhouetted by the kitchen chandelier lights behind her. Uncle Joe spoke no words; he only signaled the boys with a jerk of his right thumb that meant to get into the kitchen, *post-haste*. As the boys filed in, led by Tommy and Sean, Aunt Katy drew upon her best histrionics to effect a baleful stare.

"Where'ya been?" queried Uncle Joe, as if he didn't know.

"Drive-in," answered Tommy, knowing he was the focal point of the inquisition.

"Whad'ya see?" asked the very composed father.

A Long Farewell

"Frankenstein," said Tommy, knowing his dad could care less.

During these preliminaries, Matty noticed that the razor strap that had always loomed menacingly on a nail above the big cast-iron sink in the kitchen was missing. He had heard tales of its punitive use, but he considered them more mythology than fact, until now. With this discovery, even his sleep-deprived dullness was no protection from the terror of what lay in the torments of the two-and-a-half-feet of three-inch-wide leather that he now saw draped over one of the kitchen chairs. After some perfunctory exchanges with all the boys, Uncle Joe told them to line up a few feet from the bottom step of the long staircase and banister that rose gently from the spacious foyer up to a small landing and then a few more steps up to the second-floor hallway. Matty, who was always last in everything, was most pleased to be of such low station in this circumstance. Tommy, of course, was first in line, followed by Sean, Colin, Danny, Patty, and Matty.

"Grab your ankles," boomed Uncle Joe.

Whoosh, thwack, went the razor strap.

"Get to bed!" roared the husky-voiced patriarch.

Tommy, who Matty decided had easily received the most potent swat, conducted a vigorous massage of his buttocks as he bee-lined up the stairs, but as a practiced recipient of these cowhide delights, he had stoically taken the leather without a whimper.

Sean was next, but unlike Tommy he had imposed no monk-like rule of silence upon himself.

Whoosh, thwack, went the razor strap.

"Owww!" he bellowed, as he too sampled the balm of massage therapy between the foyer and the second floor.

Colin, Danny, and Patty took their purgatorial turns with mostly the same reactions, although once in the hallway upstairs, Patty made the absurd claim to the other four: "Didn't hurt."

Now it was Matty's turn, and he did his best with a quivering lip to bend his tiny bottom toward his towering tormentor like the five big boys had done before him. A quick study of the drill, he placed his hands on his ankles without directive but cast a furtive glance at Aunt Katy, who was biting her lower lip to restrict the laughter that was threatening to take control of a beautifully freckled face framed by thick red hair, a bit disheveled now from time on the pillow.

"Are you sorry?" boomed the judge, jury, and executioner.

"Yesss!" came the quavering response from a throat so dry and strained it could barely blurt the word.

With that came a temperate swat on the rump that was meant to teach but not to hurt, coupled with the boisterous directive, "Now, get to bed, you little rascal!"

Up ran Matty to join the others who had not seen the mitigated ferocity so unlike that delivered by their implacable magistrate. They could only stand in absolute awe of the little fellow who had endured his corporal punishment with such a stiff upper lip.

"Did he whack ya hard?" asked the inquisitive Patty.

"Oh, yeah!" said the little trooper.

"Did it hurt a lot?" asked the now-respectful Danny.

"Oh, yeah!" said the little martyr.

"Did you cry any?" asked the doubting Tommy.

"Oh, no!" said the little Spartan."

All six boys repaired to their cots in three bedrooms and pondered the evening's events. The five older boys were pretty much in the mental unison that while the adventure was something of a Pyrrhic victory, the thrill of watching *Frankenstein* free of charge more than compensated for the tingling they continued to feel in their still-rosy rumps. Little Matty's pre-slumber reflections, however, were briefer and mixed. He reveled in the presumed bravery of his valiant response to the unspeakable pain, but he went to an uneasy sleep imagining a hideous monster and a ghastly specter chasing him across an endless railroad trestle.

A Long Farewell

Years later as a high school teacher, Matty would draw upon Uncle Joe's humanity as empirical evidence of the truth in Portia's "The Quality of Mercy" speech, rendered in William Shakespeare's *The Merchant of Venice*. He envisioned his Aunt Katy as the eloquent Portia.

The Penguin

The hand of God is the promise of my own, [...]
The spirit of God is the brother of my own, [...]
All the men ever born are also my brothers,
And the women my sisters.
—Song of Myself
Walt Whitman

He had no given or surname as far as we knew, and he had no dignity or pride as far as we cared.

Each weekday around five o'clock, he departed the city transit bus that ran up and down Sycamore Drive, north of and parallel to Oxford Street, and stopped at the ludicrously named Emerson Avenue, the rough and rutted conduit that connected Sycamore to Oxford. He managed the lowest step of the trolley bus with a kind of acrobatic hop because his legs were too short to negotiate the distance to the pavement with just a casual extension of his foot. Exclusive of the hottest summer days, he was typically mantled in a black trench coat that barely cleared the tops of his squeaky wingtips. His chapeau was always a black fedora, and his white shirt, juxtaposed with his dark suit, only slightly reduced his sinister aspect. His long, pointed nose and his teeter-totter gate gave him the appearance and bearing of a waddling bird. He was hardly an inch over five-feet tall, but his swarthy countenance and curly black hair made him appear formidable. He invariably carried a brown valise in his right hand and, rain or shine, a black umbrella in his left. In this mode and fashion he traversed the distance from the bus stop on Sycamore, down Emerson, across Oxford, and over an alley to the back yard of his modest home on Ruskin Lane.

A Long Farewell

For obvious reasons, we called him "the penguin" while we harassed him from our bicycles and roller skates as he crossed Oxford Street on his way to the alley and beyond.

"Hey, Penguin, ya wanta ride? Hey, Penguin, ya wanta fish?"

On snowy winter days we'd pelt him with snowballs, and he'd do his best to effect a jocular response while increasing his pace and accentuating his waddle. We knew he took no pleasure in our attentions, but as long as we kept a safe distance, we felt justified and secure in our mean-spirited, no, our despicable behavior. One day, when I was about ten or eleven and our street-runner groupthink had become nearly epidemic, we actually followed him *en masse* to the fence and gate he had to pass to enter the alley running behind his home on Ruskin Lane. By this time our collective courage had become greatly inflated, and our insults had become boundlessly vicious.

"Hey, Penguin, don't crap in the alley. Hey, Penguin, bird shit really stinks."

Either from sheer frustration or incalculable pain, he turned abruptly that day and withdrew from his suit-coat pocket what resembled a small pistol and pointed the object directly at us while issuing some unintelligible words that were likely a hybrid of English and some European language. We turned on our heels and ran like the mindless mob that we were, screaming, "He's got a gun! He's got a gun!"

That evening we told our parents of his armed intentions, and they, of course, called the cops. After questioning the penguin, who was actually Pyotr Romanovitch, the police said that the so-called gun was only the man's tobacco pipe. He and his invalid wife were Russian immigrants.

Pyotr Alexander Romanovitch had emigrated from Petrograd, Russia with his young wife, Anna, in August of 1915, about a year-and-a-half prior to the Russian Revolution in early 1917. He was twenty-two and Anna was nineteen. Pyotr had recently completed an accounting program at Moscow State University, and his parents urged him to take his new wife to America and avoid the gathering storm. Diminutive, and even in his youth quite unattractive, Pyotr's appeal to Anna was his dogged determination and his uncommon kindness. Processing through Ellis Island, both Pyotr and Anna found menial jobs in food service for nearly three years before a friend of a friend alerted Pyotr to a job opening for a bookkeeper in the Midwest. Hired sight unseen on the strength of his cover letter and university credentials, Pyotr took Anna by train from New York to Cincinnati. After several miscarriages Anna settled into a quiet melancholy before being diagnosed with a deteriorating lung condition in 1952. Pyotr, in the meantime, remained through the years in the same modestly paid position as an obscure bookkeeper for a medium-sized firm in the center city.

When the police came to our house after their contact with the Romanovitches, they told me and my parents, as they had told and would tell the other miscreants and their parents, that Pyotr and Anna were good and gentle people who wanted only to live their lives peacefully and to allow others to do the same. Naturally, when they learned the details of my scurrilous participation in the abuses of Mr. Romanovitch, my parents lambasted me in the hottest kind of terms. My positively livid father actually said, "I wouldn't a blamed 'im if he had shot ya!" Suffice to say that from that time forward, I no longer troubled Mr. Romanovitch, but seeing him sally down gravelly old Emerson Avenue, even after I had moved on to cars and girls, continued to buttress the notion of a penguin seared so permanently in my brain.

Growing sluggishly into marginal maturity and becoming gradually aware of my self while navigating through high school and college in the sixties, I would, on occasion, recall most poignantly the lemming-like behavior of my childhood. Few of my egregious improprieties would cause me more private shame and chagrin than the memory of my involvement in the torment and ridicule of Pyotr Romanovitch, a long-suffering human being.

Perhaps my earliest recognition of the situations I would, over the years, find analogous to the abject humiliation of Pyotr Romanovitch was that day on the playground of Saint Agnes Grade School when I was thirteen. Eddie Polemous had been encircled by a group of eighth-grade boys, some of whom were my friends, and Aiden McPhillips, whose father was a wealthy industrialist, was leading the increasingly voluminous chant: "Ed-die's the rat-fink! Ed-die's the rat-fink!" Eddie had had the unbridled temerity to suggest to others that Aiden had actually participated the day before in the massive snowball attack from above upon the motorists below who were slowly climbing and descending the steep and treacherous Peach Street, which ran adjacent to the escarpment that formed one of the boundaries of St. Aggie's expansive playground. Since Aiden had categorically denied any involvement in the bombardment during the inquisition conducted by our stern principal, Sister Frances Catherine, anyone's suggestion to the contrary after the commensurate penalties had been meted out upon the marksmen would be ruinous to the heretic. Aiden, you see, was basically untouchable. Unless he was found holding the smoking gun, or in this case the melting snowball, no accusations levied upon the scion of one of the parish's biggest donors would be given credence. Eddie Polemous, of course, had stood shoulder-to-shoulder with McPhillips, as they and the rest of us had rained snow-packed mortar shells down upon those "sorry assholes" who were trying to maneuver the slippery slope. As for myself, I stood cravenly by and watched Eddie run first at one tormentor and then another before bowing his head in the tears caused by the chants and the emasculation caused by the tears. When the bell ending the noon recess recalled us to our classrooms, McPhillips marched in front of his minions like the conquering Achilles. How vividly did that Eddie Polemous episode bring to bear my shame in later years, both for my common cowardice of that incident and for my previous penguin persecutions.

As a ne'er-do-well high school student, I often found myself as a tangential or reluctant participant in my contemporaries' cruelties, but being the social nonentity that I was, I had neither the status nor the fortitude to protest or prevent them.

Riding each morning in an old Ford sedan with five other guys into the hub of the city to attend our all-male, private high school, I would frequently hunker down in the backseat when we reached the stop light at Fifth and High Streets, and the all-area forward on the basketball team, who could ridicule anyone in the school with impunity, went derisively into action. In front of the theater at that intersection, an Ichabod Crane-like man sold the morning newspapers, and with a palsied gate and gestures he would approach the waiting cars while stammering, "P-p-papers. P-p-papers." Only periodically did he make a sale, and most drivers and passengers looked straight ahead in the obvious discomfort that people sometimes feel in the presence of the handicapped. The all-area forward, however, would seize the moment to display his theatrics. Springing adroitly from the shotgun seat, he would preempt the approach of the vendor and mimic and mock him with exaggerated movements and tones, stuttering, "P-p-papers. P-p-papers." He'd be back in the car before the light changed to green, and the others would laugh raucously while I smiled sheepishly to hide my shame and pain. My shame, of course, was derived from my tacit approval of the cruel mockery of a gangling vendor, whose only fault was to be neurologically damaged, and my pain was derived from the recollection of the equally abhorrent abuse of a shy immigrant, whose only fault was to be born into a body and countenance that invited ridicule from fatuous children and condescension from patronizing adults.

Throughout my career as a high school teacher, I have been frequently reminded of Pyotr Romanovich, not only in my observations of student cruelties but sometimes of teacher carelessness as well. In addition to their inadvertent insensitivities, high school students are, of course, notorious for a click mentality that often manifests itself in the antagonistic censure of those who either march to a different drummer or fail to meet the physical and intellectual templates of "the chosen." Songwriters, novelists, playwrights, and poets have all attended to the trauma caused by a high school student's social rejection or physical abuse. Advice columnists and child psychologists write volumes about scorned pariahs and bullied victims almost daily in newspapers and periodicals, but nothing reveals the pain inflicted upon teenagers by teenagers like standing before them in a classroom or observing them in the hallways.

To this day I am not certain if any singular influence drew me to teaching as a profession or English as a subject of preference. Quite likely, the inspiration of former teachers or the intriguing nature of word arrangement drove me to the professional field and the specific subject, but like Nick Carraway, the narrator of *The Great Gatsby,* I regard myself as one of the most honest people I know. So, I must acknowledge that my choice of teaching English is most likely grounded in my very limited options, being as I am neither physically imposing or intellectually superior, but I can say unequivocally that I have for much of my life made a study of people and believed that I could make them better, even if I was clueless in regard to self-improvement.

Early in my career, I was teaching in a very large suburban high school that was adjacent to a metropolitan school district. As such, it was a melting pot of upper middle-class students and those less financially advantaged who were trying to escape the futility, violence, and apathy of the inner city high schools. Owing to the dichotomy of the classes and races and the enormity of the school population, students were inclined to seek their character clones in interests, abilities, appearance, and popularity.

One of the semester-long classes I taught was an

advanced composition course, open to the enrollment of skilled sophomores, juniors, and seniors. One of my students in that class was the somewhat abrasive and cerebral-palsied Helen Meckstroth, who was wheelchair-bound and had to be moved from room-to-room by student volunteers who benefited from their kindness by being dismissed from class five to ten minutes early and thus were able to use any surplus time for restroom or locker visits or whatever personal needs they had or imagined. Helen had a wonderfully bright mind locked in a severely ravaged body.

As each term progressed, Helen's classmates became more and more reluctant to assist her, partly because of the seemingly negative image they perceived in the act, partly because of the seemingly decreased advantage in the early departure, and partly because of the seemingly wary mien manifested in Helen's attitude. Toward the end of one class session late in the term, I was petitioning for a volunteer from an increasingly noncompliant pool of transporters when, quite surprisingly, Helen turned in her wheelchair located directly in front of my desk and announced, "Sophomores need not apply." Muffled sniggers of sarcasm rippled like a stadium wave across the classroom with the collective sentiment being, "And who wants to push you anyway, you uppity bitch!" While the usually petulant Helen visibly stunned me, I was most disappointed by the other students, who, I felt, should have been more magnanimous even in the face of a handicapped classmate's truculence. I was forced by circumstances to "volunteer" one of my go-to students who provided the assistance under the duress of my pleading expression.

Ultimately, however, I was the greatest offender in the class, notwithstanding my efforts to the contrary. About a week or two after Helen's caustic comment, I had reserved the last twenty minutes of a class period for students to begin work on their final essays of the semester and for me to get a head start on the large volume of paper grading I was facing that night. Helen, as was her wont during such times, began to doze a little, but three young ladies in the rear of the room continued to whisper among themselves rather than work on their essays. Ordinarily, I wouldn't have minded as long as they weren't disturbing others, but I was tired and irritable that day, and they were distracting me. Having told them twice to begin working, my third directive was in elevated decibels and accompanied by my histrionic slamming of the *Warriner's Handbook* loudly on my desk. The noise so startled Helen that she lurched forward in fitful movements and then fell sharply to her left with only the seat belt holding her in the wheelchair. In this posture she was suspended until I raced around my desk to bring her upright. The class, of course, erupted in laughter from what resembled slapstick comedy. Helen was clearly mortified, and I was deeply ashamed of my careless dramatics. I no sooner processed my contribution to Helen's pain than I remembered my participation in Pyotr Romanovitch's torment. No matter the years, the penguin would remain at my elbow.

Until this morning, I have, for some time, been able to suppress most of my disturbing memories of the penguin, only now and again giving him a cursory thought. Today, being Saturday, I have been taking my leisure with the morning edition of *The Daily Journal* and following my nearly scripted reading of first the headlines, then the sports section, and then the interior articles, including the human-interest stories. Only recently have I begun to read the obituaries and their attendant articles, largely because I find that more and more of the names are of my former classmates' parents or my classmates themselves. Accompanying the obituaries this morning is a brief column bearing the headline: "Bookkeeper leaves estate to C.M.C." In my morning haze I actually skimmed past the text, moving ritualistically to the listing of all the local deaths in the surrounding counties. There, near the bottom of the list, was the name Romanovitch, Pyotr A., 101.

John Hagan

The penguin, who I had assumed had been long gone, had just recently died. My eyes now flew to the column regarding the bookkeeper. In it the staff writer detailed some of Pyotr Romanovitch's life and the approximate value of his estate. He mentioned Pyotr's late wife Anna and referenced the kindness of his caregivers. The Children's Medical Center had yet to determine its use of the funds, but a spokesperson was quoted as saying that a playroom would be designated as the Pyotr and Anna Romanovitch Room.

As I put down the paper, I began to reflect upon the ramifications and irony of Pyotr's gift. A childless man tormented by an untold number of children leaves his entire estate to the benefit of children. Perhaps Pyotr was saying he forgave those who had abused him and, by extension, Anna; but I childishly hoped that he was saying he forgave me specifically for his humiliation.

The Romanovitch article triggered a stream of poignant questions. What of the newspaper vendor? Did he find a way to forgive or to cope? What was his safe harbor, his place of refuge from the world's cruelty? Was his seemingly befuddled gaze at the all-area forward's mockeries only a veneer that allowed him to sell papers in the face of countless other abuses? Could he see that I cowered in the back seat of the Ford, hoping the light would change and put a temporary end to his ridicule and my shame? What of you, Eddie Polemous? Did you see me that day standing idly by in that moment of your classmates' unconscionable scorn? Do you remember my face in particular, staring blankly among the pawns who were aping their agitator? Have you erased that playground ignominy from your memory or simply dismissed it as one of the perils of childhood? And you Helen Meckstroth, why your frequent petulance in response to benevolent acts, albeit reluctant or specious? Perhaps you were saying in effect, "I may have been dealt this lousy hand, but I'll never give in. I'll not beg; I'll not grovel; I'll not be beholden. I'll have my pride, no matter the compromising

34

circumstances!"

Forgive me, Pyotr and Anna, Helen and Eddie, and you the Vendor. My faint heart and flawed character gave you pain begotten of my cruelty, my cowardice, or my impetuosity. The penguin has this day given me further pause from his very grave. As the melancholy Dane laments in *Hamlet*, "I have shot my arrow o'er the house and hurt my brother."

A Dish Room Experience

Studies serve for delight, for ornament, and for ability.
They perfect nature, and are perfected by experience;
[But] studies give forth directions too much,
Except they be bounded in and by experience.
And they teach not of their own use;
But that is a wisdom [...] won by observation.

—Of Studies
Francis Bacon

Bilious steam issued from the entrails of the groaning leviathan, as it purged its contents of scalding bowls, cups, plates, and silverware. Jimmy watched in awe as the nimble dish-room worker retrieved the hospital tableware rapidly and placed it seamlessly on to an adjacent cart. The worker barely glanced from the pronged conveyor that pitilessly delivered load after load, fed into the monster's mouth by another worker. The ambient temperature was over ninety degrees, and Jimmy was already perspiring, just from watching the process under the passive gaze of Ursula Hospital's cafeteria supervisor.

Having recently graduated from an all-male high school in Cincinnati, Jimmy Nolan was starting his first day as a cafeteria worker in the dish room and its adjoining chambers on this early June morning. He had been accepted to and had enrolled in Xavier University in Cincinnati, but before classes began in the fall, he needed to earn some tuition money in the summer. With the exception of the cafeteria supervisor's, his was the only white face in the area, and even in his insulated naiveté, he didn't mistake the sly glances of askance shared by those who would soon be his co-workers. The supervisor was Sister Angelina Schmidt, whom he would rarely see again for the remainder of the summer. Obviously preoccupied with other matters, she was conducting this very perfunctory orientation as quickly as possible before scurrying off to something more cerebral.

"James, if you have no further questions, I'll leave you in the capable hands of Mr. William Sanders and Mr. Jerome Creech, who'll break you in a bit today."

She remained quite formal in her use of all the workers' given names.

"Uh, no, Sister, I don't think so."

Jimmy was so intimidated by his new surroundings and imminent associates, the only question he really had was, "Where's the nearest exit?"

"Very well! William and Jerome, I'll leave Mr. Nolan to you."

Sister Angelina exited the dish room quickly, and Jimmy turned his eighteen-year-old face to William Sanders, who had cut the monster's power and stopped its roar to hear the comments of the departing supervisor. He gave Jimmy a broad grin that revealed a full mouth of gleaming choppers, punctuated by a luminous gold incisor that practically lit up the room. Jimmy didn't know whether to interpret the smile as that of a Cheshire cat or of a benevolent mentor. It was neither on this first day; it was just Willy's natural demeanor.

"Just call me Willy. I'm kind of unofficially in charge when Sister's not around, since I've been here the longest."

"I'm Jimmy. Jimmy Nolan."

Jimmy extended his hand and took into his a heavily cal-lused, dark brown one that was still quite warm from the intense heat of the china and silverware. By this time, Jerome Creech had come around from the feed end of the dishwashing machine to introduce himself.

"I'm Jerry Creech."

Jimmy shook another hand that was not as dark brown but equally callused. Willy looked to be about thirty years old and Jerry about twenty-two. After some cordial exchanges, Willy reminded Jerry and Jimmy that it was already 8:40 and they still had most of the breakfast dishes to wash from the patient floors, and the cafeteria's dishes wouldn't stop coming in until it closed at 9:00. Willy grabbed an apron for Jimmy, who, as summer help, wouldn't be issued the personalized gray-shirt-and-pants uniform worn by the full-time workers.

"Ya ready to start?" asked Willy, as Jerry headed back to the feed end again.

"Sure!"

"Now, I gotta tell ya these dishes are really hot, so it's gonna take some gettin' used to before ya get the hang of it."

Willy positioned Jimmy at the retrieval end of the machine and pushed the stainless steel cart next to the neophyte. By that time, Jerry had restarted the motor, and with a signal from Willy, he began feeding the soiled tableware into the machine. Using the slowest and most ineffective setting on the conveyor, Jerry waited for the predictable signal from Willy to halt the process. Shortly thereafter, the conveyor delivered the first dishes from the finger-burning sanitizing phase of the machine into Jimmy's schoolboy hands. The heat of the tableware was almost unbearable, and within a minute or so several dishes and cups had fallen into the bin beneath the conveyor, forcing Willy to gesture Jerry to stop the motor. Although Willy was assisting Jimmy by stacking the dishes and depositing the utensils, the college-bound boy simply couldn't keep up with even the slowest pace of the conveyor. Only the pain in his hands exceeded the embarrassment Jimmy felt for his ineptitude. Willy, however, remained patient and told Jerry to increase the pace, and then he did his best to assist Jimmy by pulling some items from the prongs of the conveyor as he continued his stacking and stashing.

The three workers labored steadily until they stopped to eat around 12:30, about forty-five minutes beyond their usual lunch-hour time and without any mid-morning break.

Throughout the morning Jimmy became only slightly more proficient, and by noon his hands had become crimson and throbbing, but he had begun to feel that he was at least more help than hindrance. Willy and Jerry repaired to the locker room to eat brown-bag lunches, which, of course, Jimmy had not thought or known to bring. After buying some peanut butter crackers and a Coca-Cola from the vending machines outside the cafeteria, Jimmy joined the others. When he arrived at the locker room, Jimmy found an enormous black man stretched on a bench with his back propped against one of the locker doors. He was smoking a cigarette and pulling on a 16 oz. bottle of RC Cola.

"This here's Leroy," said Willy matter-of-factly to Jimmy. "He works in the pan room all day because he's too damned big to let in the dish room with humans."

Willy slapped right hands with Leroy as he passed the Goliath on his way to a locker to change his shirt.

"Hi! I'm...Jimmy Nolan."

Leroy Thurman nodded obligatorily and regarded Jimmy suspiciously over the blue-lens Benjamin Franklin sunglasses he wore at all times. Jimmy extended his hand, and it absolutely vanished in a huge paw attached to a gargantuan arm belonging to a 6'7" 320-pound body. Leroy's thighs measured more than Jimmy's waist, and his head was as big and round as a soccer ball.

"Hi, yourself, Peewee," said the giant in a voice that was two or three octaves lower than what Jimmy might even have predicted from the small continent of a body.

As Jimmy would later discover, pan-room duty was straight out of Dante Alighieri's *Inferno*. The room itself was about eight-feet wide by about twelve-feet long, and it was equipped only with a rectangular stainless steel sink that stylishly featured two rusty spigots. It had no windows or any discernable ventilation, and on summer days the temperature in the room could easily reach one hundred degrees. To this stark chamber were cart-delivered stacks of steel pans that were six-inches deep, three-feet wide, and four-feet long. They were caked with the seared remnants of chicken, pork chops, macaroni, casseroles, and all manner of foods baked in huge convection ovens. Pan-room duty meant taking delivery several times per day of a shipment of these encrusted containers and scouring them with an Ajax- or Comet-laced ball of interlocking metal ringlets. To say that an eight-hour shift of this Herculean labor was beastly would be to say that a root canal was mildly unpleasant. The job was typically assigned to those who were strong of back, impervious to heat, and otherwise unemployed. Leroy met all the criteria, but strangely enough, he seemed to prefer the job to other assignments in which he had to work with fellow employees. Leroy shared the pan-room schedule with a part-timer who was as slender and lithe as Leroy was beefy and muscled. Sundays were the worst day of the week, being heavy on hospital visitors who frequently took at least breakfast or lunch in the cafeteria.

Around 1:10, Jimmy followed Willy and Jerry back to the dish room as they drifted slowly from the locker room after a lunch break that was shortened by thirty minutes because of Jimmy's training-day blunders. The lunch dishes and silverware from the cafeteria and patient floors would be waiting already or arriving soon for Willy and Jerry, regardless of the albatross they had had to bear in the morning. The remainder of the day and week was marked by a steady improvement in Jimmy's skills and an increasingly easy rapport with his co-workers, notwithstanding a substantial number of broken plates, saucers, and cups that hadn't made the journey from Jimmy to the stacking cart. At the end of the shift on Friday, Jimmy caught the city transit bus home, and as he drifted into a reverie induced by the hum of the motor and trolleys, he reasoned proudly that he was doing something truly meaningful for the first time in his young life. No, it wasn't virus research, but it was something that needed doing, and it was done in the company of an ethnic group with whom he had had virtually no previous experience and with regard to whom he had borne numerous misconceptions.

Jimmy Nolan was an Irish Catholic boy who had been reared in an all-white, middle-class family and neighborhood, and he had been educated in an all-white, Catholic grade school and high school. As such, he was not exactly of the so-called privileged class, but he was certainly much more advantaged socially, educationally, and financially than a large segment of the city's population.

As Jimmy progressed in his dish-room skills, both feeding and retrieving, his acceptance among the black men became delightfully obvious, developing to the point where repartee flowed spontaneously and good-naturedly. He gained immeasurable masculine status one Friday after work in a foot-race challenge from Jerry, whom he defeated on a nearby track with a finish-line lean in a hundred-yard dash, started by Willy and judged by Leroy. In fact, the summer was advancing too quickly as he approached his university life and the master's degree that he blithely assumed would follow his bachelor's in English. It wasn't until he received the call on a Saturday night in mid July that his simple life became complex. The call came to his home around 7:00, and his mother handed him the telephone.

"Sister Angelina is asking for you."

Jimmy's immediate thought was that she had just learned how many dishes he had broken since the first of June.

"Hello."

"James, this is Sister Angelina, and I'm sorry to interrupt your Saturday night, but I'm in a rather difficult situation. Neither Leroy nor Henry is able to cover the pan room tomorrow, and, unfortunately, I can find no one else to replace them. Could you do me the enormous favor of taking the pan-room assignment tomorrow morning? I can pay you time-and-a-half for the overtime hours."

Having watched Leroy and Henry on occasion, the mere thought of pan-room duty made Jimmy sweat with loathing and fear, but he simply couldn't disappoint this kind and genteel nun.

"Sure, Sister. What time?"

He knew what time. He just wanted her to have to say it.

"Well, I need you to be there at seven to take the first pans, but you can still catch the six-o'clock Mass in the chapel if you'd like."

"Oh...yes."

"Thank you, James! I do appreciate your cooperation. Goodbye, now!"

"Goodbye, Sister."

Jimmy punched in at 6:55 a.m. on the ground floor of Ursula Hospital, having foregone the six-o'clock opportunity to meet his ecclesiastical obligation. He sauntered down the long hall to the cafeteria area and eased into the pan room, which was illuminated by a bare, hundred-watt light bulb located just above the tub. The first pans arrived from the kitchen about 7:10. Relentlessly supplied with stacks of cumbersome pans, Jimmy loaded each one from the cart into the long sink and scrubbed and scoured it with the powdered detergent and steel-ringed scraper. Each pan took about fifteen minutes, the more belligerent ones about twenty. By 11:30, he was sopping wet from perspiration and suds, but he had finished the last of the breakfast supply. Looking every bit the drowned rat, he glanced out the door of the pan room to see a twenties-something black girl in a standard-issue green, hospital worker's dress, staring at him curiously but not kindly. He had seen her several times throughout the summer but had suppressed his prurient thoughts about her curvaceous body and luscious face. She was about 5'7" with supple, dark brown hair; her face, arms, and legs were a creamy chocolate color. She stared at him for at least ten seconds, and he just stood there dripping soapsuds and sweat on to his squishy shoes. He smiled pleasantly and started to address her, but she turned abruptly and walked away.

Jimmy spent his lunch hour alone in the men's locker room, thinking of the girl whom, he now admitted to himself, he had been watching whenever he could for several weeks. She worked as a server in the cafeteria, and he had discovered through stealth that her first name was Priscilla. Why, he wondered, had she stopped to stare at him? The answer had three possibilities: because he played the proverbial village idiot, because he looked like a bleached and shrunken Leroy, or, preposterously, because he enchanted her with his striking good looks. To his recollection, he had never had more than the briefest exchange with a black girl, never mind a flirtatious encounter. Did black girls even like white guys? What would he say to her even if he had the chance? He had seen her smile a few times, and she revealed teeth so perfect and white they looked like a mannequin's. She was all soft curves and velvety skin, and Jimmy, in spite of his inhibitions, wanted her far more than he cared to admit, even to himself.

At 3:35, Jimmy Nolan trudged down the hall to the time clock to punch out from the longest working day of his life. He had probably lost at least five pounds from his slender 155-pound frame, and his sodden pants and shirt were clinging to his legs and chest. His fingers were raw from the steel-linked scraper and powdered detergent, and his lower back was aching from the daylong burden of the bulky pans. Most everyone from Ursula's day shift had punched out already, and the hallway near the time clock was practically empty. As he turned limply from the time clock, he collided with Priscilla Cooper, who had arranged for the accident by a surreptitiously established proximity.

"Oh, sorry!" blurted the human dishrag.

"You should be, you fool! You've gotten me all wet!"

Before Jimmy could make further amends, she smiled and said, "You're Jimmy Nolan, aren't you."

"Yeah, and you're Priscilla…"

"Cooper."

Jimmy just stepped aside as Priscilla punched out.

"You're the boy who's headed for Xavier next month, aren't you."

"Yeah, I guess, if I ever dry out."

Priscilla laughed a deep, sexy, almost lascivious laugh that made Jimmy want to embrace her right there in the hospital hallway. They stood and talked for about fifteen minutes, exchanging the typical kinds of introductory information, as other hospital workers drifted by or punched out quickly.

It was almost four o'clock when Priscilla looked at her watch and said, "Wow! It's getting late. I'd better get going."

"Yeah, I've gotta catch a bus, and they don't run very often on Sundays."

"I could give you a ride. Is it far?"

"Yeah, it's miles from here and I couldn't let you do that."

"Oh, I don't mind, but I'd have to stop at my apartment first."

"No, I couldn't let you…"

"C'mon. Walk with me to the parking lot. I can get you home a lot faster even if we run by my place first."

Jimmy couldn't believe what was happening. Suddenly, his fantasies about Priscilla had materialized into a real-life opportunity. She had shared with him in their brief conversation that she was 22 and that she had moved to Cincinnati from Montgomery, Alabama, at 18, leaving a home with eight younger siblings and two poverty-line parents. She had her own apartment and drove what she called an "ancient Ford." He didn't know what was next, but his carnal experiences to-date were restricted to some French kissing, spit swapping, and lewd petting with Marcy Hamner in his dad's four-door Chevy after the senior prom.

"Okay. If you're sure it's not too much trouble."

They walked together to Priscilla's car, a beat-up Ford

Fairlane with two dented hubcaps, one blackwall tire, and three whitewall tires that looked like they "had come down from Esau and Samson."' When they arrived at her apartment in a low-income neighborhood, Priscilla invited her hesitant co-worker into her modest domicile.

"Oh, I can just wait in the car. I don't mind."

"Come with me. I want you to see something."

When they stepped into what was a two-bedroom unit of a four-unit complex, a matronly seventies-something black woman greeted them warmly.

"She's still asleep. She wouldn't go down for her nap until three o'clock."

"Oh! Wow! Well, that's all right, Yolanda. I'll get her up in a few minutes."

Priscilla handed Yolanda some greenbacks and walked with her into the hallway and over to the landing of the stairway. After some thank you's and goodbye's, Priscilla walked back into the apartment to find the nonplused Jimmy standing with his mouth slightly agape.

"I'm sorry about this. I didn't think she'd still be sleeping."

"She?"

"My one-year-old, Cassandra."

"Oh!"

"Does that scare you?"

"Well, it surprises me a little."

"A little?"

Jimmy laughed nervously to buy time for his next comment.

"Uh, well. A lot, I guess."

"That's okay. Her father never took any responsibility. He followed me up from Montgomery shortly after I left, and he took off as soon as he knew I was pregnant."

"Look, I can just walk to a bus stop. I don't want to bother you anymore."

"Don't want to bother me anymore, or have anything to

do with me anymore?"

She had looked right into Jimmy's eyes, and suddenly all of his apprehensions were lost in the beautiful brown orbs that bewitched him with their sincerity and sensuality.

"Well, I guess I could stay for a while."

Priscilla offered Jimmy a beer, and together they threw back some Hudephols and ate some pretzels while waiting for Cassandra to awaken. About forty minutes later, Priscilla led Jimmy into her bedroom for one of the most exquisitely pleasing experiences he ever had or would have. Her body was everything that Jimmy had imagined, and her mastery of the situation made him feel like an experienced lover. When Cassandra finally began crying, Priscilla showed Jimmy into the nursery and introduced him to a beautiful infant girl.

Jimmy spent the next few weeks preoccupied with Priscilla and finding an excuse to walk to her apartment at least once a week. Thoughts of college and his future as an English teacher shrank from his planning as he became more and more addicted to the delights of Priscilla's body and the charms of Cassandra's antics. Their fanciful life together in the confines of the apartment was both clandestine and intoxicating. Priscilla and Jimmy seemed to wallow in what each brought to the other: for Jimmy, the splendid pleasures and companionship of an experienced, beautiful woman; and for Priscilla, the wide-eyed affections and caring of a future professional man. If the guys at work knew of Jimmy's relationship, by mid August they had given no voice to or indication of their knowledge. Still, Jimmy felt that his relationship with them had changed somehow. They were no longer the curiosity they had been to him in spite of his workplace bonding; he now felt of them, a part of them, no matter how tangentially.

On the third Friday afternoon of August and after his last day in the dish room, Jimmy walked again to Priscilla's apartment. He was to start classes at Xavier in about ten days, and he was beginning to consider full-time employment in lieu of college. When he broached the subject with Priscilla, she surprised him with her opposition to his plan. In fact, her demeanor was visibly melancholy from the time she opened the door. When he had asked her perfunctorily if something were wrong, she seemed evasive and brooding. He dismissed her mood as the result of a long week in the cafeteria. Only when she objected vigorously to his plans for employment instead of education did he fully process her anxiety.

"What's so wrong with my gettin' a job and waitin' on college for a year or two? I could help you and Cassandra, and we could be together as much as we wanted."

"I don't even want to hear you say that! Who said I need your help, anyway? You're not Cassandra's father, and you're not my husband! You're just a kid yourself."

Jimmy was taken aback and shaken. His feelings were hurt and his pride was wounded.

"I'm not a kid! I'm only four years younger than you!"

He had no sooner offered his protest than with lightning speed he realized how ridiculous his claim was. Priscilla's empirical age was vastly greater than her chronological age, and in worldly matters she dwarfed Jimmy's experiences. In spite of his absurd reasoning, she tried to restore his dignity.

"No. I'm sorry. You're not just a kid. But I'm not right for you, and you should know that."

"Hogwash! What's really wrong?"

"Nothing. I just want you to leave, now. And please, don't come back!"

Her manner had changed from demanding and authoritative to pleading and deferential. He stood for a moment and looked at Cassandra in the playpen beyond Priscilla. She was standing with her hands on the rungs, smiling at him. He left the apartment and walked to the bus line. He never saw Priscilla again.

About two weeks after he had begun classes at Xavier, he

borrowed his dad's car and drove out to Priscilla's apartment. When he knocked on her door, an old woman across
the hall opened hers.

"You lookin' for Priscilla, honey?"

"Uh, yeah."

"You a fren?"

"Yes. I am!"

"Well, honey, she moved out, enda the month. Didn't say
where she was goin'. Jist drove away in that ole Ford with
her baby."

Jimmy Nolan graduated from Xavier four years later, and
he took his first English teaching job at a highly integrated
high school in the inner city of Columbus, Ohio.   He
remained there until he took a higher paying position in the
Columbus suburbs. His life changed in many ways over the
years, but Priscilla Cooper and the Ursula Hospital dish
room remained as much a part of his essence as any of his
most formative influences. He never knew with certainty
what was troubling Priscilla on that last day, but he had a
pretty good idea.

Roughing It—Mark Twain

The Power of Suggestion

She was a Phantom of delight
When first she gleamed upon my sight;
A lovely Apparition, sent
To be a moment's ornament; [...]
A perfect Woman, nobly planned
To warn, to comfort, and command.
—She Was a Phantom of Delight
William Wordsworth

He could see from the newspaper picture that she was still beautiful. The prominent cheekbones, dark brown eyes, and tousled brown hair were perfect complements to a beguiling smile enhanced by teeth that fell a bit short of an orthodontist's billboard ad but made her seem real and natural. Her picture was one of ten provided by *The Daily Journal* of the area's Women of the Year. She was, in this group of mostly middle-aged women, as she had been years ago among college girls, a "dove trooping with crows."' She had been selected on the basis of her philanthropic work in conjunction with her and her husband's law firm that did extensive *pro bono* work among indigents in the city, particularly minorities. The director of the local chapter of the Urban League, who was quoted from a ceremony held two years before as he had presented her the League's outstanding service award, had nominated her. In the course of *The Daily Journal's* three paragraphs delineating her achievements, an excerpt from the U.L. director's remarks included: "Paula is truly altruistic; she eschews recognition for her many off-the-record efforts on behalf of the less financially fortunate, and she works tirelessly to represent those who would otherwise be without legal advice."

John Hagan

After reading the information about Paula Daniels, Mike Mangan lowered the newspaper in pensive recall. He'd been told by someone long ago that Paula had met her husband, Robert Daniels, shortly after she had passed the bar exam and joined the law firm where he was also a cub attorney, earning his stripes in contract negotiations. They were both catalog-model attractive and, blessed with frightening legal acumen, were on the fast track to prodigious professional and financial success. After about five years with the firm, however, they struck out on their own and formed their own firm of Daniels & Daniels, Attorneys-at-Law. Some lean years followed, along with two children, but once Paula and Rob gained some traction, they became known throughout the area as two of the most formidable negotiators in the state. Mangan stared out the window from a booth in the diner where he had just finished his breakfast, and he sipped on a rapidly cooling cup of coffee while he indulged himself in some bittersweet reverie.

He was late, as usual, for his eight-o'clock English Composition 101 class on the third floor of old Saint Joseph's Hall. As he raced up the wooden steps, well worn in the middle by the countless students who had trod there for over a hundred years, he was careful to avoid slipping on the dampness created by those who had arrived in a more timely way on this very rainy and cold, late-November morning. By the time he entered the rear of Room 312, the big hand on the clock in front of the room was just past the 2 and the little hand was a touch past the 8. Professor John Fuller regarded him over the top of his horn-rimmed glasses and a dog-eared copy of Sinclair Lewis's *Dodsworth*, from which he had been reading a particularly soporific passage, and shot Mangan the penetratingly baleful stare he reserved for the miscreants who arrived at his lectures late, specifically those who did so repeatedly. Mangan took his usual seat to the left and rear of the classroom, flipped open his copy of the Lewis novel, and checked his folder to see just how wet his expository essay, due at the beginning not the end of class, had become during his dash from a distant dormitory. He was hoping that this third essay of the semester would be returned to him garnished in something less than the seemingly total contents of a red-ink pen and rated at something greater than the F and D- that had defiled the two priceless forerunners of his latest effort like graffiti might debase Leonardo da Vinci's *Mona Lisa* or Sandro Botticelli's *Birth of Venus.*

As Fuller lectured on and eventually ignored the distractive student, Mangan drifted once again into the comfort of his almost tangential involvement in the class, and he focused his attention upon the feminine pulchritude that was perched three seats ahead of him in the row of student chairs to his immediate right. The singular factor that drove Mangan to attend an eight-o'clock class on at least a fairly regular basis was Fuller's star pupil who seemed as disinterested in Mangan's presence as she was indifferent to his desires. She did, occasionally, cast what could be loosely construed as a furtive glance over her shoulder at Mangan, but for the most part she appeared so engrossed in Fuller's gospels and her own contributions that had Mangan not arrived habitually and intrusively late, he would likely have been to her an absolute nonentity.

Her name was Paula Blair, and Mangan had learned during the first day's introductions that she was a graduate of a private school for girls in Columbus and was, as she had said, "earnest in my desire to improve and refine my writing skills here at Bordeaux University." Mangan didn't know why she preferred to call herself "Ernest," but he decided in that epochal and defining moment that she was really, really sexy. As a graduate of a huge all-male Catholic high school in Cincinnati, Mike Mangan was about as facile in his approach to girls as he was skilled in his writing of prose. Paula Blair, however, intoxicated him with delusions about their being romantically linked. Mangan had from his earliest interest in girls been especially attracted to beautiful legs.

John Hagan

Although his equally oafish and boorish high school buddies were self-described "breast men," who rated girls on the basis of whether they were "really stacked" or had "bodacious ta ta's," Mangan had never been particularly intrigued with girls along those lines. With the introduction of Paula Blair into his provincial life, however, he discovered that the female posterior could be as voluptuous and alluring as a pair of shapely gams. True, Paula's classroom apparel typically included a fashionably short skirt that maximized the appeal of panty hose stretched tightly over well-formed calves and luscious thighs that she crossed and re-crossed repeatedly during every class session. But while the legs did tease and delight, the frequent shifting in the chair of the most curvaceous buns he had ever seen was most distracting to his otherwise burning interest in Fuller's lectures on the art of Sinclair Lewis, essays from the rhetoric, and chalkboard examples of student errors in usage, grammar, diction, mechanics, spelling, punctuation, and the always captivating parallel structure.

Mangan was suffering the common syndrome of the sixties college freshman: academic shallowness compounded by the lack of sustained self-discipline, productive study habits, and efficient time management. Exacerbating these shortcomings was the sixties emphasis upon Comp 101 as a kind of litmus test to determine the propriety of a freshman's continued enrollment. The additional "turn of the screw" in Mangan's composition woes was the fact that he was positively smitten by the intellectual and physical charms of Miss Paula Blair, who had by late November never acknowledged his mere existence with even the most perfunctory smile.

Toward the end of the class on that dank November morning, Professor Fuller reminded his pupils that as was noted in the syllabus, the fourth and final essay of the semester, a literary analysis of *Dodsworth*, was due on the last day before Christmas break and would be returned to them graded during the lame-duck period before examinations in mid January. They would, of course, have their expository essays returned to them before submitting their literary papers. As they began to depart the classroom that day, Mangan wanted desperately to make some overture of his interest in her to Paula, but first he had to submit his paper to Fuller, and that came with another admonition regarding his recurring tardiness. By the time Mangan reached the hallway, Paula had left Saint Joseph's Hall.

Throughout the remaining class meetings before Christmas break, Mangan's resolve to engage Paula in conversation became weaker and weaker, particularly as his fears increased that she would rebuff him cavalierly, if not derisively. Added to his confidence problem was the fact that his third essay had been returned to him with another D-grade and crawling with textual corrections. Although he managed a respectable 78% on the tough *Dodsworth* test, the result was hardly enough to compensate for the disastrous grades on the weighty descriptive, narrative, and expository essays. His hopes for at least a C grade for the course lay with the literary analysis essay and the final exam.

Mangan spent most of the Christmas break in Cincinnati worrying about five semester grades and pining for one female classmate who ostensibly had little or no knowledge that he even shared the campus.

On a snowy January morning when scarf- and parka-clad Bordeaux University students trudged like zombies across the frozen and bleak Midwestern campus, the students in Professor Fuller's eight-o'clock class ambled into Room 312 for the last regular-class meeting before exam week. Fuller had little to do that day other than to remind students of the material to be tested on the final and to return their literary analysis papers. Before returning the papers and dismissing his students early, however, he announced, "I am rarely surprised at this stage of the semester by the quality of a student essay, nor am I inclined to read aloud an essay in its entirety. But, notwithstanding what I

John Hagan

anticipated from this student, I am impressed beyond my expectations."

Mangan was by this time almost swooning from the exhilaration born of the belief that he had finally turned a corner in his writing and had struck compositional gold.

Fuller continued.

"Before I dismiss you today, I would like to read the essay of Miss Paula Blair, who, in spite of what I have come to presuppose from her as a first-rate submission, has written an analysis of Lewis's novel that extends far beyond the norm for a freshman writer."

As Fuller began reading, Mangan's colossal disappointment turned quickly to burning rage, but as he processed Paula's written words, he realized just how profoundly stated her analysis was and just how profoundly superior to his sophomoric blather her insightful observations were. At the end of the reading, the students applauded what they recognized as a rare talent in their midst. When the rest of the papers were handed to the departing students, the dumbfounded Mangan returned to his desk and pondered the devastating D- on his final effort. As he read the commentary on his paper through the blurred lenses of a defeated and solitary figure in a now-quiet and darkened room, he looked up to see Paula Blair standing almost in silhouette in the doorway, staring at him. He immediately shoved the paper into his folder and offered the feeblest smile. She said nothing yet, but approached him from the doorway.

As Paula sat down in the student chair next to him, she said in a mellifluous voice that was almost equal in its charm to her extraordinary beauty, "How come you've never said hello to me, Mike Mangan?"

"Uuh..."

"We've been in this class together since early September, and you've never once even acknowledged my presence."

"Well, you've never..."

"How many times did I have to turn in my desk to look at

54

you without drawing Fuller's attention?"

In one fell swoop Mangan went from devastation to triumph, but he was so confounded he was unable to seize the moment advantageously.

"Well, you're so damned smart I just didn't think you'd have any interest in what I'd have to say. Besides, I've tried to find the right time or place to speak to you, but something or someone always got in the way."

"I find that hard to believe."

"Well, right now in fact I'm so embarrassed by my last paper, I can't find the right words to say."

"There are no 'right' words, and if you'd have given me the time of day during the semester, perhaps I could have helped you with your papers a bit while we were getting to know each other."

"Right."

"You know, you're really not too hard to look at, and when you've bothered to offer something in class, it's surprisingly interesting. Out there, but interesting."

"I doubt that you and the rest of Fuller's finest would've been real interested in my brilliant observations."

"You're too hard on yourself, Mangan, and you don't give other people much of an opportunity to take you seriously. Anyway, now that I've forced you to speak to me, maybe we could get together once in a while."

"That'd be fine with me."

Mangan didn't want to tell her that his days at Bordeaux were probably limited to the next week's exams, but what he did want to tell her was that nothing in the world would please him more than to be with her for the rest of his life.

"Well, all right then. Let's get through exams and then see what happens. You could call me, you know. I'm living in Marianist Hall, and there's a phone desk at the end of each floor."

"Okay."

She stood up, and for the first time since she had walked

back into the room, Mangan took notice again of her astonishing beauty and uncommon poise. She almost literally took his breath away. She reached out and put her hand softly on the side of his face.

"You shouldn't underestimate how sexy you are, Mike Mangan, by just being a really nice guy. See you next Friday."

She walked out, and Mangan found himself torn between sheerest joy and harshest fear. He had finally had a close encounter with the girl of his fondest dreams, only to realize that his days at Bordeaux and his proximity to her were most likely limited.

The next Friday was the last day of exams, and the Comp 101 exam was Mangan's last of the day. It covered a full range of the semester's material, including sections on *Dodsworth*, the rhetoric, *Warriner's Handbook*, and notes from the lectures. Although he had been preoccupied with thoughts of Paula, Mangan had studied hard, and he believed he had done reasonably well on the exam, but the cumulative effect of the essays would be most damaging. Paula was one of the first to finish, and he was one of the last. Surprisingly, however, she was waiting for him on the landing between the third and second floor.

"How'd ya do?"

"All right, I guess."

"Good! I just knew you would."

"Well, I'm sure you knocked the socks off it."

"Listen, I've got a ride to Columbus later tonight, so I won't be around tomorrow. But if you'd like to get together for a while, I've got a six-pack cooling behind the curtain on my window sill."

"You've got beer! I can't believe that the goddess of composition would ever touch the stuff."

"Mangan, you'd probably be really surprised by what I'm willing to touch."

"What time?"

A Long Farewell

"My ride's leaving around nine, so why don't you come by Marianist around seven, and we'll hike over to Woodland Park for a while."

"It'll be cold."

"We'll be okay."

At 7:00, Mangan picked up Paula, and she spirited the beer and a bag of pretzels out of the dorm in a shopping bag. It was quite cold outside, but for some reason, the temperature wasn't a problem. They found a secluded park bench, popped open two beers, and, after some mindless small talk, gave up the beer and practiced some passionate groping and kissing for an hour and a half. When they finally had to return to campus, Paula started forward but Mangan pulled her back. She gazed at him under disheveled hair with her beautiful eyes in such a way that she seemed to know intuitively what he knew viscerally: she would not see him again. The die was cast. He would not compile the grade-point average necessary to return to Bordeaux University. She kissed him softly. It was the sexiest kiss he ever received.

"You know, Mike Mangan, you're much better than you think."

When they returned to her dorm, there was so much departure activity that they had little opportunity to say anything meaningful. A voice in the dark yelled, "Hurry up, Blair!" So Paula raced up the brick stairway to the front door and then turned and smiled. Mangan simply stared.

Mangan spent the remainder of the winter, all of the spring, and most of the summer working for a friend's father's construction company. The experience taught him to appreciate the value of a college education. With the money he saved from that laborious work, he enrolled at a small, all-male college in Indiana. He majored in English and went on to teach high school English, earning an M.A. on a part-time basis at Indiana University. After two failed marriages and as many children, he was on the brink of retirement when he received the mailer from the English

John Hagan

Department at Bordeaux University, announcing the conference for advanced placement English teachers. In spite of
his imminent retirement, as the A. P. English teacher and
department head at his high school, he felt an obligation to
attend. Besides, returning to Bordeaux with two degrees and
a highly successful career in the classroom would be a satisfying vindication of his erudition.

The conference ran for two days in late May on a
Thursday and a Friday, and because the Friday afternoon
sessions lasted until 4:30, Mangan had booked a room at the
Marriott for two nights. When he walked into one of the con-
current sessions late Friday, he noticed that the distinguished looking, iron gray-haired presenter seemed familiar.
He introduced himself as Dr. John Fuller and said, "I've been
teaching here at Bordeaux since McGuffey published his first
book." Mangan was not only delighted by such an ironic circumstance, but he found Fuller to be an absolutely splendid
and dynamic speaker with a marvelous wit and fascinating
anecdotes. What a difference a perspective made. He wanted to introduce himself after the session, but a host of others
engulfed Fuller with questions. That evening Mangan had
dinner at a well-known steak house near campus and then
drank a few beers at the Marriott bar before collapsing on the
queen-sized bed in his room.

On Saturday morning, he picked up a copy of *The Daily
Journal* outside the diner before going in for breakfast. When
he read the headline in Section B, "Ten honored at the convention center tonight," he barely took note before turning to
the Sports Section. After reading why his beloved Reds had
blown another three-run lead in the ninth to lose to the
Cubs, he returned to Section B with greater interest.

He recognized the face before he even read the name.
The haunting eyes of Paula Daniels, nee Blair, seemed to
gaze at him knowingly just as they did that night in
Woodland Park.

When he returned to the present from his reminiscing,

Mangan reread the third paragraph. It revealed that Paula's award would be bestowed posthumously and that her husband Rob would be accepting it on her behalf. A drunk driver had killed Paula six months before.

In a hushed voice made raspy by emotion, Mangan said to the picture, "You know, Paula Blair, you're really not too hard to look at, and you made me believe that I was better than I thought."

`*Romeo and Juliet*—William Shakespeare

The Apparition

Everywhere near the creek,
Which here had a margin of lowland,
The earth was trodden into mud
By the feet of men and horses.

—Chickamauga
Ambrose Bierce

A man stood behind and off to the left of an antebellum farm house and stared across the field of timothy that ran in an L-shape to the rear and the right of the house. The field began to the left of him at the meandering creek and ended at the three-acre stand of old-growth trees that separated the ten-acre field of timothy from a five-acre field of corn. Holding his stare was what he thought was a surge or swell in the thick trees that bordered the creek where it ran parallel with the field until the timothy turned its attention to the corn.

The sun was high in the hazy sky at 12:37 p.m. on that sultry 19th of July 2013. The soft breeze, along with the carpenter bees that bounced off the window screens of the front bedroom, had roused the man slowly to consciousness around 7:00 a.m., but by midday it had died completely. Now, without so much as one leaf seeming to stir in any of the ninety-acre farm's many stands of trees, the day had become what the older farm folk had called "close." The man had been completely awash in idle musings when, as he turned toward the house, the peripheral vision of his left eye birthed the nascent thought that he was being watched from the direction of the creek and tree line that bordered the timothy. He focused intently on the spot that had arrested his attention. He saw nothing but the trees, and he was reminded of Gertrude's words in *Hamlet*: "Nothing at all; yet all that is I see." As he scanned the field between himself and the tree line, he detected a delightfully unfamiliar fragrance, but the only movement he saw was the white butterflies that densely populate crop fields in the deep dominions of summer. The only sound he heard was the clamor of those errant cicadas that had missed Nature's memo forbidding their ceaseless cacophony until early August. What was it? Had his delinquent left eye sent him a prankish message?

Notwithstanding the day's otherwise tolerable conditions, an eeriness engulfed the spot in the tree line that at a considerable distance seemed ever so briefly to shimmer before the man's eyes. In the absence of further evidence, he decided to return to the front porch of the farmhouse where he had been guzzling beer and inhaling popcorn while preparing another query letter to another publisher who would summarily dump his manuscript on to the slush pile. He had received so many rejections of his contemporary novel that his ego had been battered beyond recovery. The combination of the beer and the humidity had made his T-shirt and shorts stick to his skin from perspiration, and he felt the wooziness that washed over him when addled with ale and standing in the sun.

As the man stepped toward the house, his sneaker popped a small round object from the turf that formed the divide between the grass of the dooryard and edge row of the timothy. He paid it no heed initially, but after turning for a second look at the tree line, he was compelled to retrieve the object and examine it more closely. As the man rubbed the dirt from what the heft and shape suggested was a flat, circular stone, his serendipitous prize resolved itself into a rusted, Hunter pocket watch. The cover and crystal were long ago gone, as well as the hands and numerals, but the stem remained attached, fused in place by rust. The watch was far too corroded to open the back, but the hinge was still discernable.

John Hagan

"I'll be damned!" said the slightly intoxicated Kevin Coughlin.

Owing to his intemperate ways, Coughlin might well be damned, but from this fortuitous discovery, he was about to enter a dimension that would result in an extraordinary and never-to-be-forgotten experience.

***

Eight-year-old Annie Powell was sitting against the paling fence just outside the "house in the holler" trying to decide whether the amphibian she held in her hand was a frog or a toad when, on that day in mid July of 1863, she heard the pounding of many horse hooves beyond her vision on the creek road that ran past the house. Annie knew instinctively to move to cover before the riders cleared the trees that obscured her presence, so she quickly repaired to the creek bed below the riders' line of vision. She had tucked the frog or toad into the side pocket of her bib overalls, and she was peering over the creek bank when approximately thirty or forty ragamuffin riders stormed into the clearing by the little house. The commotion, caused by the saddles of the dust-caked and sweaty mounts, the sabers and chains of the bearded men, and the orders barked by the dashing leader, seared a graphic image in Annie's memory for a lifetime.

Commanding this band of sublime but tattered warriors was an imperious looking horseman who approached the front door of the little house. He sat upon an enormous black mare that stood over sixteen-hands high, and with his prepossessing bearing and on his imposing mount, he might have claimed to be Zeus himself. As the only formally uniformed trooper, he wore a broad-brimmed black hat that was festooned with a magnificent feather. His tunic bore several brass buttons down its dusty front and one embroidered star on its high collar. His long coal-black hair was swept behind his ears, and he wore a neatly coiffed mustache and goatee.

A Long Farewell

Leaning down from his lofty saddle, he hollered into the partially opened front door, "If anyone's in thayr, commone out. We only need drectshuns totha Powl fahm. Ah'm lookin' for mah cuzin, Annabelle Powl."

Waiting in abeyance, the rest of the troopers' horses stamped and snorted while intractably impatient. Annie, of course, knew that itinerant field workers used the little house only at planting and harvest time. She also knew that Annabelle Powell was her mother Annabelle Morgan Powell, who lived with her family on the other side of the creek and up a long lane that was not visible from the creek road because of the dense summer foliage.

"Ah sed, commone out now; we meanya n'hawm."

Believing in her safety, Annie hollered from the creek bed, "There ain't nobody in there; it's just a field-hand house."

With that, she scrambled up the embankment and revealed her identity to the astonished but amused horse soldiers.

"I'm Annie Powell, and that's my mama you're huntin'."

The commander reined his horse around, doffed his hat in an ostentatious manner, and intoned, "Brigdeer Genral John Hunt Mogan at ya suhvice, miss! Canya kinely drectus to ya mutha's domicile?"

"Well, if you mean to her house, of course I can! She lives with my papa and my brothers and sister and me right up that lane on the other side of them trees and creek. I can take ya, if ya want me to."

"Ah'd be ohnud if ya'd rahd with me astrad Black Bess, miss."

And with that he extended his arm and swung the saucer-eyed Annie up behind him. He gave an order to his lieutenant who repeated it to the rest of the troopers, and with Annie aboard he led the thundering brigade through a break in the tree line, and they splashed through the creek bed and galloped around the front corn field to the mule-and-log-cleared lane that provided ingress and egress for the farmstead.

As this band of raiders and its pigtailed escort made their way up the long dusty lane, General Morgan could see from a distance of about 100 yards that two people sat on the front porch of the clapboard farmhouse. Near the house, the lane's high banks gave way to a verdant barnyard that allowed the entire party to rein in together in the expansive area that merged with the dooryard. The T-shaped and hip-roofed house was assisted beyond the breezeway by a summer kitchen that allowed for cooler meal preparation during the sweltering months of July, August, and September. The porch ran the entire breadth of the front of the house about three feet above ground level. Under it was a crawl space, covered by a decorative lattice that had been breached on the left side by a child-sized portal. Four, five-foot-wide oak steps that were roughly plumb, but well worn in the middle, provided access to the porch from the front yard.

By the time Morgan had approached the porch with Annie behind him, a man and woman had risen from their straight chairs and stood by one of the columns supporting the tin roof. Their countenances were characterized by the kind of amazement that seizes small-town children when a traveling circus selects their main street as part of its itinerary. The presence of what was some of the finest light cavalry in American history in their barn and door yards left the man and woman with their mouths agape.

Morgan sat on horseback before the porch, and with his sinewy left arm lowered Annie to her feet. The girl sprang up the steps and squealed, "Mama, this here's General Morgan, and he says he's your cousin!"

The puzzled amazement on Annabelle Powell's face turned to a studied scrutiny and then to an ecstatic recognition.

"Johnny, it's you!"

She dashed down the steps and ran to Morgan, who by this time had stepped down from Black Bess. He embraced

64

his cousin in a bear hug that drew her nearly a foot from the grass.

"Annabelle, ah doan b'lieve ah've seenya since ah enlisted foah thah wah withtha Mexigans. Mutha tole me a few yeahs ago thatya were in this aarea, and bein' this cloze, ah jist hada tryda fineya. A fahma southa heah tole me we could fineya if we follod tha creek road 'bout two mals nowtheast. But with 'is bein' a Nowthana, ah did'n know if he was sendin' us straight intatha gunsats of fedral troops. Lawd, it's gooda see ya!"

"Johnny, I can't tell you how glad I am to see you. It's just divine providence that you found us, but you're right; there's a company of federal troops bivouacked outside Hillsboro, just north of here, and scouts could've easily seen your approach, had you gone much farther."

Burl Powell had by this time descended the stairs and was standing at his wife's elbow. He was a large, robust man of unquestioned Union loyalties, being a homegrown Ohioan, but his wife's family members were Southerners, and her allegiances and relatives would be respected on his land. Besides, he could never quite transcend his belief that whether Yanks or Rebs, they were all just American boys.

Annabelle Morgan Powell was nearly two years John Hunt Morgan's junior. Her father, the brother of Calvin Morgan, the general's father, had moved with his wife and family from Huntsville, Alabama to Lexington, Kentucky in 1833, about eighteen months after Calvin had done so before him. As a result, John and Annabelle became quite close as children. When, at age 21, John enlisted in the Army to serve as a cavalry private in the Mexican-American War, their contact with each other had been all but broken. At age 20, Annabelle had traveled to Southern Ohio for a friend's wedding and met and married in a whirlwind romance the affable but plain-speaking Ohio farmer R. Burl Powell. She loved her bucolic life, but she sometimes longed to revisit the bustle and flurry of Lexington.

"Johnny, I've forgotten myself. This is my husband Burl Powell."

The two men shook hands warmly and vigorously, but each was suspect of the concealed wariness of the other.

Burl turned and pointed toward the assembly of men. "That boy down by the barn admiring your troopers is our eldest, Thomas Harold. Tommy'd join the Army tomorrow if his age didn't prevent him."

He had directed Morgan's attention to a strapping eleven-year-old who looked like he would join the Union or Confederate Army, as long as he could exercise his already perfected abilities to ride and shoot.

Annabelle continued the family inventory.

"For the life of me, I don't know where B. W. and Rosie have gotten to. B. W., where are you?"

She hollered in the direction of the summer kitchen, but the response came from under the porch.

"We're under here. He ain't gonna shoot us, is he? I'll give them marbles I pinched back to Jamie Robbins, but I didn't take no puries, anyway."

Morgan broke into a spasm of laughter.

Burl took control.

"B. W., you and your sister can just get yourselves out here, at once!"

From the breach in the lattice crawled a dirty-faced but cherubic three-year-old girl, followed by a sheepish six-year-old boy whose sandy hair seemed to have been recently bowl cut.

Morgan saluted them formally before breaking into disarming and contagious laughter.

"Ah do b'lieve ah've forgotten mahself as well."

He gestured to his young lieutenant who was waiting patiently still on horseback about twenty feet from his commanding officer.

"May ah present mah aide-de-camp, Fust Lieutent Bas'l T. Breck'nridge of Dayt'n, Kentucky. Lieutent Breck'nridge is

jist outta Wespoint, Class a '62. He'll be mah second'n com-
man en route to owa rendezvous with Cap'n McCreary and
Maja Duke's commans."

"Pleezed ta meet all of ya!"

"Have you been with the general long?" inquired Burl
Powell.

"'Bout nine months, sir."

"Do you have a girl back home, Lieutenant?" asked
Annabelle.

"Oh, yes, ma'am! We're gonna be married, soon as we
lick these Yankees. Uh...sorry, Mr. Powell."

"That's all right, Lieutenant. We'll just consider this
gathering our little armistice."

"Thank ya, sir. Ah jist get a little carried away when ah
talk about mah Lucy. We've known each other since grammar school, and with mah goin' off to the Point and now with
this war, we've just had to put off our weddin' for so long."

"I'll bet you think of her often, don't you," said Annabelle.

"Ma'am, every time ah get this out and look at and smell
her picture and read her words, ah jist wanna ride back to
Dayton and hold Miss Lucille Jane Collier in mah arms."

He withdrew a beautiful watch from his trouser pocket
and held it up for all to see.

"She gave it to me as a graduation present."

Annabelle couldn't resist. "What's the sentiment say,
Lieutenant?"

"Annabelle!" exclaimed her husband.

"Well, ma'am, let's jist say that to me they're the most
beautiful words ever written. And they're what'll see me
through to the end of this war when ah return to her."

"Well said, soldier boy, well said!" blurted the giggling
and blushing Annabelle.

The next hour or so was spent with General Morgan sit-
ting on the porch steps drinking lemonade, reminiscing with
Annabelle about their lives in Lexington, getting to know the
Powell family, and making oblique references to his Ohio and

John Hagan

Indiana raids. Meanwhile, his small detachment of men watered their horses from the barn trough, filled their canteens from the lift pump, and rested themselves under the shade trees. They would, over the next three or four days, rejoin the larger detachments of Morgan's command along their way to the Ohio River, where they hoped to cross over into West Virginia. Among those detachments were two groups of approximately 700 men each, commanded by Captain C. W. (Charles Wilson) McCreary and Major John A. Duke. They and other splinter groups would meet Morgan at strategic locations in Southern Ohio and return to the South, having conducted raids that had pillaged property, burned bridges, stolen horses, commandeered supplies, and killed and captured thousands of federals. Their return to Dixie would not go unchallenged.

When the rested cavalry remounted their steeds, General Morgan bade farewell to his cousin in a tender embrace, and he whispered in her ear, "Pleze pray forus, Annabelle. Ah feah fowthese boys. Thayr beards belie thayr youth."

"You'll remain in my thoughts, my dear Johnny!"

To Burl Powell, Morgan turned and said, "Suh, may we take owa leave thruya back field? Doin' so'll saveus considerable tahm."

"It's only orchard grass, General. Be my guest, and may God put a speedy end to this ungodly war!"

After Morgan gave his orders to Lieutenant Breckenridge, Annabelle, smiling impishly at the general, hollered to the junior officer, "What time is it, Lieutenant?"

Beaming, Breckenridge proudly withdrew his pocket watch and announced, "It is now fourteen hunerd hours of the time that flies, Mrs. Powell."

With that, he took the lead of his men toward the back field and haphazardly replaced the timepiece in his watch pocket. A few feet into the orchard grass, the treasured gift from Miss Lucille Jane Collier dislodged from his pocket and fell under the hooves of the ensuing horses.

A Long Farewell

***

Kevin Coughlin returned to his writing table on the screened-in front porch of the farmhouse. He had been examining the corroded watch curiously as he walked from the field, but now he set it on the table and turned his attention to his query letter to Random House. After tinkering a bit with the phraseology, he went to the kitchen for another Amstel Light and then shuffled back to the porch. Contrary to his present semi-inebriated state, Coughlin generally remained in good physical condition. He prided himself on looking younger than his fifty-two years, and he pumped iron three days per week on his weight bench and ran laps three times per week on the running path that roughly encircled the farm. In addition to his two ex-wives, he had had a few long-term relationships with other women, but his carousing had exceeded their tolerances as well. He held a Bachelor of Arts in English from Ohio University and a Master of Arts in Teaching from Miami University, but he had rarely remained in a high school teaching position for more than a year or two. He was currently employed as a sophomore English teacher at Fairoak High School, which was about ten miles from the farm that he had received along with the mortgage payments in a settlement from his second marriage.

***

In the late morning of July 19, 1863, the aggregate assembly of General Morgan's regiment of about 2,500 men was confronted with the conundrum of trying to cross the swollen Ohio River at Buffington Island or turn and face a vastly larger force of federal regulars under the commands of Generals Hobson and Shackleford. Exacerbating Morgan's predicament were two federal gunboats patrolling the Ohio. Deliberation became purely academic when Morgan took a frontal attack from General Henry Judah's Home Guard.

During the battle, approximately two hundred of Morgan's men succeeded in crossing the Ohio, but nearly seven hundred were captured and subsequently sent to the appalling Camp Douglas Prisoner of War Camp near Chicago. Morgan escaped north with most of the other survivors, but he too was overwhelmed and taken prisoner on July 26 near Salineville, Ohio.

Nearly one hundred of Morgan's 2nd Kentucky Cavalry were killed at the Battle of Buffington Island, and that number included a young lieutenant who had become distracted by the loss of a prized pocket watch given to him by the love of his life. Lieutenant Basil T. Breckenridge was slow to horse when Judah's forces struck, and he had barely gained control of his right stirrup when a rifle ball tore through his aorta and killed him almost instantly at 12:37 p.m. In the melee, Morgan saw his esteemed aide fall, and from a perspective gained by the ravages of war, he knew instinctively that the wound was fatal.

***

Kevin Coughlin made a few more adjustments in his letter to Random House and then stood to stretch his legs. Without really knowing why, he picked up the pocket watch again and found himself walking back to the spot next to the timothy where he had made the discovery. Again, his attention was drawn to the trees where he had detected something vibrant. After turning the watch in his hand for another look at the back side, he looked again at the trees and beheld a nebulous figure on horseback staring at him from about eighty yards across the field. So startled was Coughlin that he dropped the watch. He retrieved it quickly, but by the time he stood erect again, the horseman had vanished, leaving Coughlin with only the watch and the subtle scent of the now-familiar fragrance.

"Holy hell! I've had way too much beer."

He started back up the slight grade from the timothy field, through the barn and door yards, and turned around twice to re-examine the tree line. Nothing. He walked up the stairs of the porch, entered through the screen door, and collapsed on the couch.

"Ya have mah watch, sir," said the young Confederate officer who was seated upon a beautiful sorrel gelding that was standing on the grass in front of the porch.

Kevin Coughlin eyed the soldier suspiciously.

"What makes you think it's yours? You're just a damned Reb who'd say anything to fleece a man of a fine watch."

Coughlin looked down at the glistening watch. The second hand was moving with Swiss precision across the black Roman numerals that were juxtaposed against the immaculately white face. The ornate small hand was a little past the twelve, and the even more ornate big hand was a little past the seven.

"Ah'm tellin' ya the truth, mister. Mah fiancée, Miss Lucille Jane Collier, gave me that watch as a present when ah graduated from the United States Military Academy in 1862. Ah lost it in the back field of this farm a few days before ah was slain at the Battle of Buffington Island. We were gonna be married, but some infernal Yankee put a musket ball through mah chest right here!"

He put his finger through a hole in the front of his blouse.

Coughlin stood up from the couch and stepped toward the edge of the porch.

"What right do you have to show up here to demand this watch that may not even be yours?"

"Ah haven't come to demand the watch. Ah've come to tell you that you found it almost to the hour and the minute 150 years after ah was killed in the battle. If you'll open the back, you'll find a beautiful girl's likeness, scented with jasmine perfume."

Coughlin paused for a moment and then took his thumbnail and lifted the back of the watch. There, in blond tresses, was the beautiful Lucy, and an enchanting fragrance greeted his nostrils.

The soldier recited the inscription while Coughlin read silently from the watch:

> This watch keeps time for you.
> My heart keeps love for you.

Coughlin stared blankly at the tattered remnant of a gray Confederate uniform. Slowly his eyes met the anticipating gaze of the lieutenant.

"Whatya want from me?"

"Mah Lucy never married, and she died of the typhus in 1866. She's buried in the churchyard of Mount Olive Methodist Church in Bellevue, Kentucky. Please take the watch there and lay it on her tombstone."

"That's all?"

"That's all."

"Why?"

"Your askin' tells me you wouldn't understand the reason if ah told you."

The soldier reined his mount to the left and disappeared from Coughlin's sight.

Around 4:30 p.m., a determined housefly began landing on Coughlin's cheek and eventually irritated him from his hops-and-barley-induced nap.

"Sonofabitch! I've gotta stop drinkin' in the afternoon. Won't be long before I'm playin' ping-pong with Napoleon."

He was still clutching the corroded watch. He swung his feet to the floor of the porch and stared at the relic. He had to know. Working with a penknife and a needle nose, he pried the back of the watch open, breaking the fused hinge as he did. No picture was found. Only some disconnected words were barely discernable:

> watch   for you.
> heart keeps love

He was on his way to Bellevue, Kentucky early in the morning.

He set the two pieces of the watch on the tombstone of Lucille J. Collier and walked to the wrought-iron gate of the old churchyard. When he turned for a last look, the faint smell of jasmine graced the air around him, but the watch was gone.

Coughlin never returned to Bellevue or shared his experience with anyone. Some things are simply too cryptic to be believed, understood, or appreciated by others. Occasionally, on a breezeless and sultry summer day, while running the path at the farm, he felt the presence of Brigadier General John Hunt Morgan and First Lieutenant Basil T. Breckinridge.

Night Call

Though she [...] was far from complimentary,
She was of about my own age.
She seemed much older than I, of course,
Being a girl, and beautiful and self-possessed;
And she was as scornful of me as if she had
Been [...] a queen.

—Great Expectations
Charles Dickens

Leisel was nearly as pretty as the day he first saw her in the hematology laboratory at Queen of Martyrs Hospital. She was beginning her clinical experience that day as a senior, medical technology major at the nearby University of Cincinnati, and he was in his third summer of lab work earning money for his senior year as an English major at a small college in Indiana. As only a summer-trained tech, Declan was quite limited in the tests he was authorized to run, but for him the job also provided a dynamite way to hit on the student nurses and younger R.N.'s, who for the most part thought he was an insufferable idiot with an incurable case of horns aplenty.

***

Declan Shay was filling a rare day-shift assignment and sitting at his microscope reading a differential when the new crop of med tech students being oriented by Dr. Angus McFarland, the dazzlingly brilliant, spontaneously sportive, and grandly irascible pathologist, entered the hematology lab one Monday morning in early August. There were eight of them, seven attentive girls and one studious-looking guy.

74

A Long Farewell

She was a stunner: tall, blond, and blue-eyed, but she glanced at him with a look so disdainful he felt lower than the nasty Trichomonas he reported occasionally when reading urine microscopics at night in the chemistry lab. By the time the group moved on to the blood bank next door, Declan had re-counted the same neutrophils, lymphocytes, and monocytes three times. He spent the rest of the summer in a vain effort to make inroads with Leisel Stenrude as she and her classmates moved daily through the various laboratories. McFarland was not ignorant of Declan's interest in Miss Stenrude, and he made every effort to keep the randy tech as busy as possible. McFarland had an eye for beauty himself, and in his heavy Scotch brogue he would commonly comment to Declan about a winsome lass he had admired in the cafeteria at lunch. Once, with Declan assisting him in the tissue lab, the pathologist pointed to an illustration of a uterus and said in the most formal of tones, "Ah, theritis Daclin, that from which man coomes and spands the rast of 'is life tryin' t'gat back in."

It wasn't until Declan was home for Christmas in December and taking a night call for one of the registered medical technologists who wanted Christmas Eve off that Leisel was dropped into his lap like a gift-wrapped present from Santa. Night call for the unlucky med tech at Queen of Martyrs who drew it on a holiday meant sleeping in the coop-like room on the fifth floor on an institutional cot with starchy pillowcases and sheets. It was always beastly hot up there no matter the weather, and the tech could count on at least one call per night from the emergency room, asking for a complete blood count or a type and cross-match of two or three units of blood, a lengthy procedure that would prevent any real sleep. The one-person shift ran from 11:00 p.m. to 7:30 a.m. and fell between the 3:00 p.m. to 11:30 p.m. night crew, who handled pre-op patient C.B.C's and E.R. calls, and the 7:00 a.m. to 3:30 p.m. day crew, who handled the more sophisticated testing for the medical floors.

The call came from McFarland about 12:15, just after
Declan had fallen asleep. The pathologist was calling from
the morgue, and he wasn't in a festive mood.

"Who's this?"

"Declan Shay, Doctor."

"What the hell're ya doin' up there? I thought Fanley had
noight call. Areya 'ome for krestmas, Daclan?"

"Yes, I am, Doctor. Rob gave me a call, and I kind of need
the money, so I said I could come in for him. Sister Anne
Charlotte approved the change."

"Well, dammit, why wasn't I infarmed. What th'ell'm I,
chopped laver?"

McFarland could have cared less who was taking night
call. He was just vexed because he had to come in himself.

"Well, I need some 'elp down 'ere in the margue. Canya
get down 'ere queckly?"

"I'm on my way."

By this time Declan was fully awake and recalling the
accounts of some of the pre-med guys who also worked as
summer lab techs and had had experiences with McFarland
in the morgue. Declan, who had never even been in the
morgue, had a mixed feeling of dread and anticipation. He
called the E.R. secretary to let her know where he'd be and
then hauled ass.

When he arrived at the morgue on the ground floor of the
hospital, he knocked, and after almost a full minute
McFarland opened the door only partially. He was dressed in
a surgical gown and rubber gloves, and he peered around the
door and asked if Declan had ever assisted him before.

"No, Doctor."

"Avya aver obsarved an autopsy befar?"

"No, Doctor."

"Avya aver ben in the margue befar?"

"No, I haven't."

"Abab!"

Declan could tell that McFarland was beginning to soft-en, and for the first time since the pathologist's call, he was really hoping he'd be allowed to assist.

"Well, duya thankya can 'andle bein' 'round a cadaver?"

"Oh, sure!"

Even before McFarland fully opened the door and brought him in, Declan could see over the pathologist's shoulder the head and upper torso of a nude body lying on a table. As they passed through the anteroom, McFarland made a point to pull out two or three of the refrigerated drawers in the wall to show the first-timer a few bodies waiting the arrival of the undertakers. Another drawer revealed an amputated leg. There was a purpose to this introduction that Declan would understand about three hours later.

What greeted Declan as he entered the inner morgue area was indelibly recorded in his mind. The body of eighty-four-year-old Sarah Sandhurst lay on a stainless steel table that reminded Declan of a dentist's oversized spit sink with water swirling around the four-inch sides. Her head was propped on a small metal tripod, her brain having already been removed and now accenting an adjacent porcelain-topped table. Her chest had been opened in the standard Y incision, and the sternum had been cracked, the ribcage pulled apart. Sarah Sandhurst was simply an object for analysis. Whoever she was or whatever she meant to family and friends was irrelevant in this circumstance. She was to be examined and scrutinized with a respectful but strictly clinical detachment.

Declan Shay was surprised by his own composure. He was neither stunned nor distressed, yet. McFarland seemed to sense Declan's need to stare, to marvel, to process it all. For at least a whole minute, the pathologist said nothing.

"Daclan, arya gowin' ta be ulright?"

"Oh, sure!"

"Than, let's gat started. I've ban colled away from a krestmas party my wife and I're 'avin', and I need ta retarn as soon as possible. The marticians wantta take the body 'arly in the marnin', and thus the need fora poost at this ungodly hour."

"I see."

"What I wantya tado ista stand on the opposite side of the table and hand me anstramants and equepmant on the shalves behind ya as I need 'em, okay?"

"All right."

"Now I loik ta canduct a little lacture for my intarns and the pre-med students whan I'm doin' a poost. Wouldya loikme ta take ya along with me a bet?"

"Uh, sure."

With that, McFarland began removing organs and then weighing them in a hanging scale that looked much like one a butcher might use to weigh a fine filet mignon for a customer. As he did so, he proceeded with his monologue, commenting upon the condition and circumstance of each examined part. As the hour grew later and McFarland's party awaited him, the tedium seemed to take its toll on his patience for the task and his tolerance for Declan's ignorance. Once, while commenting upon a part he had removed, he said something that Declan couldn't decode.

"Splan."

Thinking that McFarland was asking for an instrument, Declan looked for something that looked like a "splan."

Having no luck, he said, "I'm sorry, Doctor. I didn't understand."

Without looking up, McFarland repeated, "Splan."

The pathologist's heavy brogue, mixed with an intensity and irritation exacerbated by the late hour, completely confused Declan. With his anxiety rising, he looked again for something splanlike. Seeing nothing that induced understanding, he said again, "I'm sorry, Doctor, I..."

"I said spleeen, dammit; I tukout the damned spleeen!"

With that, McFarland dropped the spleen into the hanging scale and took note of its weight. Shortly thereafter, he took what looked like a common butcher knife and began slicing the brain carefully into thin parcels, reminding Declan of how his father would cut a meatloaf or a roast into equal portions for everyone.

"Theritis. That's what tuk'er."

He directed Declan's tired eyes to a spot on a layer of the brain.

"Daclan, I've fanished now, and here's where ya moost come in. I samply moost retarn to what's left of the party, but there's still wark ta be done 'ere. I'm goin' ta stetch up the back of the 'ed, but whan I'm fanished, I'd loikya ta stetch up the chast cavity. Willya do that far me?"

"Uh, sure."

"In spite a the hour and sarcumstances, we moost bear in mind that we're warkin' with a human bein', someone pracious to loved ones, desarvin' ev'ry respact. Doya understand?"

Declan nodded.

After McFarland finished the back of the head with a small needle and fine thread, he showed Declan some coarse thread and a large curved needle that looked like a carpet tool. He placed all the intestines in a plastic bag, tied it, and pushed it into the chest cavity.

"Now, what I wantya tado, Daclan, ista began sewin' the Y incesion at the bottom of the Y an' wark yar way up until ya've complately closed the incesion. Later, the arderlies'll place the body in one of the refregerated compartments. I'm goin' ta leave now. Canya 'andle this far me?"

"Uh, sure."

With that, McFarland walked out of the morgue proper and through the anteroom. When Declan heard the outer door close, he looked at his watch. It was 1:45 a.m.

For about three minutes Declan remained in a fixed gaze over the grisly work that awaited him. The needle, threaded by McFarland, lay on the small table next to the body. He couldn't touch it. He began to panic as he realized that he had overbooked himself with his bravado around the pathol-

79

ogist. McFarland was gone now, well on his way to his Christmas party. Three significant phenomena remained: Sarah Sandhurst, Declan Shay, and oppressive silence. For another minute or so he lamented and cursed his situation.

"Why'd I agree to take night call for that damned Finley? Why didn't I tell that friggin' McFarland I couldn't do this?"

Eventually, however, anxiety and fear gave way to a nervous resolve born of an emerging belief that Sarah Sandhurst was counting on him to do his duty to her. He picked up the needle and thread and began sewing the flesh of an eighty-four-year-old woman whom he had never seen before this night and who neither felt the prick of the needle nor thanked him for his efforts.

About an hour later he looked at his handiwork and took pride in his recent accomplishment but felt disgust for his previous squeamishness. When he returned to his fifth-floor quarters, it was 3:15 a.m. He didn't think he could sleep, but around 5:00 a.m. he was awakened again by a call from the emergency room, asking for a cross match of two units of packed cells for a car-accident victim. By the time he returned to the lab from the E.R. with his filled vacutubes, it was almost 5:30. *Why in the hell couldn't this have come in about an hour or so later for the damned day crew to handle?* he thought. Quite possibly the physical answer to that mental question appeared in the blood bank doorway around 6:50 when the bleary-eyed Declan Shay was finishing the two units.

"You look like you've been rode hard and put away wet."

The voice belonged to Leisel Stenrude, looking every bit the *femme fatale*.

Through most of August, he had worked on his tan and hit the iron each day so he'd look his best when he arrived at the lab at 3:00 p.m. for his night shift, hoping Stenrude would give him a look as she and the other med tech students were leaving for the day, but no results. Now in December at his pasty whitest, unshaven and sleepless, she shows up from nowhere.

"Uh...do I?"

Even his voice sounded like he'd been gargling with peanut butter.

"I didn't think you could take night call. I thought you were just summer help."

"Well, I'm coverin' for Finley, who said he had a big date last night. Besides, I can handle most of the emergency stuff. I could even cookbook through a red-cell indices if I had to."

He was lying, of course, but she wouldn't know.

"Couldn't you get your own Christmas date? I thought you were supposed to be such a hound."

She was starting to rankle him and she knew it.

"Well, in the first place, I just got home from school a few days ago, and I'd been pretty busy with papers. In the second place, what makes you think I'm such a 'hound'?"

"Most of the student nurses have ya pegged."

He had begun to lose his focus on the two units he was labeling, so he tried to concentrate harder on his task. Leisel, however, continued to stand in the doorway as he called the E.R. for the pick-up. He was trying to do something with his unkempt hair before he turned to face her again on his swivel stool.

"So, what are you doing here, Miss Stenrude? Aren't you on Christmas break?"

"I decided to work for pay during the holidays, and with so many hematology regulars off for Christmas Day, I'm here as part of a skeleton crew. Shouldn't be too much to do today though."

Even in a white lab coat at this hour of the morning she looks like Venus, he thought.

With her hair pulled back in a ponytail and tied with a lavender ribbon, her big blue eyes reminded him of the boulder puries he and other guys coveted in the marble games he played as a kid. Declan was generally rather glib, and he fancied himself as something of a wordsmith, but in this situation he was all but verbally inert.

"Well, didya have anything interesting last night?"

For the first time her tone was something less than mocking and her gaze something less than condescending.

"Actually, for me there was."

Leisel didn't ask what at first, so he didn't offer anything. After a minute of an abbreviated Russian standoff, she finally yielded.

"All right, what was it?"

He explained how McFarland had called him down to the morgue and what he had had to do. Something in the explanation of his ordeal or in his regard for Sarah Sandhurst must have intrigued Leisel, but he really wasn't trying to score any points right then. Anyway, he was sure she was immune to any of his machinations. During the course of his account, an R.N. had picked up the two units, and a couple of the day-crew people had drifted into the hematology area. Leisel had said little, but she had laughed at his discomfort with McFarland, partly because she'd done a tap dance or two herself to avoid his awesome wrath or one of his brutal critiques. After Declan briefed the day-crew person in the blood bank, he walked into the hallway and headed for the elevator down to the ground floor to punch out.

As he pushed the DOWN button, a voice behind him said, "Hey, Shay."

He knew it was Leisel before he turned.

"Where ya headed?"

"Home, I guess."

"To your parents' house?"

"Yeah, I'm just a poor struggling college boy."

Janie Patterson, a twenty-seven-year-old day-crew technologist with great buns and boobs, had called him that a couple of times, and he liked the image.

"Well, I'm staying at an R.N. friend of mine's apartment this week because she's in Lauderdale."

"That's great."

"Well, I know this sounds rather forward, but...if you'd like to go there now and get some sleep, I'm only working until one, and maybe I could make you a Christmas lunch before ya head home."

Declan didn't know whether the effects of a nearly sleepless night were causing him to hallucinate or not.

"You mean...you want me ta sack-out at your place?"

"If you're not okay with that, I'm sorry I mentioned it."

"No. Uh...no. I just...I just wasn't sure I understood you right."

She laughed when she said, "Well, I've had my eye on ya for some time."

"Right!"

"No. Really. You got outta here at the end of August before I could let ya know. I was pretty busy trying to keep up with things during the first few weeks."

"Busy! You wouldn't give me the time of day, literally."

"Well, you've got such a reputation as a masher."

"I do not. I'm just..."

Then she did something that pretty much reeled him in completely. Being at least as tall as Declan and thus nearly eye-to-eye, she reached toward him and lightly pushed his hair off his forehead. Then she just looked at him in a way that girls can that has ten times the impact of any verbalized sentiment. Neither said anything for a few seconds.

"Look, I've got to get back to the lab. Do you want the key?"

The question was like asking Prometheus if he'd like a coffee break from his rock.

"Uh, yeah!"

She pressed the key and street address into his hand, turned, and said over her shoulder, "You really are a masher."

"Gimme a break."

Declan arrived at the apartment at about 8:00 a.m. and

let himself in. It was a one-bedroom unit in a four-unit complex, about standard for a young nurse starting her career. Furnished with hand-me-downs, it had a homey atmosphere with all the female trappings and appointments. Although he pretty much collapsed on the couch and fell asleep immediately, he awakened about 11:30 and decided to jump in the shower. He shaved with a leg razor he found, using hand soap for lather. He even brushed his teeth with some Crest and his fingers and sprayed his armpits with some feminine antiperspirant.

Around 1:30, Leisel Stenrude walked into the apartment. Declan was toast.

***

Declan Shay was in town on a Friday night to attend a testimonial dinner for an old friend who was retiring as a hospital administrator, and he recognized Leisel almost immediately from across the spacious party room at the Marriott Hotel. He was amazed that after all these years she had remained so trim and looked so youthful. The traditional little black dress and the now-short blond hair with the Doris Day bangs contrasted strikingly. She was sipping on what looked like a Martini and talking to a handsome man in an elegant gray suit, accented by what was likely a Christian Dior silk shirt and necktie. He was about 6'2" with ruddy skin and thick silver hair, coiffed very professionally. He seemed to be doing most of the talking, but she seemed to be smiling only perfunctorily, albeit beautifully. Leisel Stenrude Allen had glanced over the shoulder of the talking suit several times at Declan, who was standing alone with a Michelob draught in his hand near the bar. Not until she locked on to his persistent stare did the nascent thought that he seemed familiar begin to crystallize for her. Declan smiled at her but took no other expansive liberties. He hadn't seen her since the end of that Christmas break so many years before when they had cohabitated in her friend's apartment for a week. She had written to him a few times from U.C. and he to her from over in Indiana, but with each of them graduating that spring and taking jobs in the fall, she as a registered medical technologist and he as a high school English teacher, they had lost contact with each other.

Declan watched her curiously as she appeared to disengage herself politely from conversation, and after greeting two or three people in the space between herself and Declan, she made her way over to the bar.

"Declan Shay?"

She extended her right hand and smiled at him in a knowing way that made the interrogative greeting superfluous.

"Leisel."

Declan's heart rate was no less than it was that morning when she had surprised him in the lab after his night call experience with Sarah Sandhurst.

"I'd looked at you several times before I realized that the guy who ravaged me for a week and then ran for the hills was standing over by the bar. You look wonderful, you rascal!"

"Me! Why do you think I've been staring at you for the past fifteen minutes? Other than the shorter hair, you're still the same sexy temptress you were at U.C."

"Stop it! No, don't stop it. You're obviously still the lovable bullshitter you were at Queen of Martyrs."

Declan reeled in embarrassed laughter and false affront.

"Seriously, what do you do? Pilates? 10K's? Weights?"

"All of the above. You?"

"No Pilates, but otherwise about the same, with some horseback riding thrown in."

"Where? The horseback riding, I mean."

"The same place I do the weight work and most of my running. A small horse farm I bought a little east of here when I retired from teachin' English."

"I heard you were teaching. Where?"

"At three different high schools in Indiana. I've been teaching comp as an adjunct at U.C. for the past year."

"Married?"

"Was. My two kids are out of college and on their own. You?"

"Divorced for some time now, but I'm still the lab supervisor at Children's. My only child, a daughter, is married and living in Lexington."

They spent most of the evening together, catching up and filling in some of the gaps. They discovered that the friend of Declan's who was retiring was Leisel's boss at Children's Municipal Hospital. Declan was struck by the impression that in spite of the years, Leisel hadn't seemed to change, and in an obviously more mature way, she was still very hot. She filled out the little black dress beautifully, and her bare arms and legs were firm and sinewy. When she walked before him to the buffet table, Declan made no attempt to avert his eyes from the still-curvy butt that did every justice to the dress. As they prepared to leave, he alone and she with a friend from the hospital, Declan didn't know how to handle the awkward goodbye. He knew he was making himself totally vulnerable and ridiculously eager, but too much time had passed not to try.

"Leisel, I know this sounds a bit forward, but since tomorrow's supposed to be a beautiful summer Saturday, I was wondering if you'd like to drive to the farm and do a little horseback riding with me."

She gave him a look that made him wish that he could yank his words from the air and squash them.

"Why, Declan, are you tryin' ta hit on me?"

"No! Actually, I was just trying to re-create your Christmas morning invitation to me a long time ago. I'm sorry if..."

Leisel broke into one of her lovely smiles and touched the side of his head.

"I'd love to go horseback riding with you. I actually do a

little riding at a stable across the river."

"You do?"

"Yeah, I do. What time?"

"I can have them groomed and ready to ride around ten."

"I'll be there in my boots and jeans."

"Boots and jeans?"

"Real humdingers!"

Declan laughed and then became pensive.

"Ya know, if I hadn't agreed to take night call for Finley that Christmas Eve, we probably wouldn't be having this conversation right now."

She smiled emotively and turned to leave but then told her friend she'd catch up. She turned again and stepped quickly back to Declan and just stood looking at him for about five seconds.

"You know what really turned me on that Christmas morning in the blood bank?"

"Nope."

"The way you seemed to care so genuinely about an eighty-four-year-old dead woman. It ran so contrary to the impression I had of you. I'll bet you've been a fine teacher."

"Not sure my students'd agree."

"Yes, they would. See you at ten, Declan Shay, you naughty Irish boy!"

Equine Magic

Riding a horse is not a gentle hobby,
To be picked up and laid down like a game of Solitaire.
It is a grand passion.

—Journals
Ralph Waldo Emerson

As Jack Sullivan stepped down from the red-bricked breezeway between the old farmhouse and the ramshackle summer kitchen, he stretched and rotated his arms in a superficial warm-up for his thrice-weekly, five-mile run around the farm. Rising only thirty minutes before at 8:15, he had slept about an hour longer than what his body clock generally allowed. Having swilled beer on the oak-floored front porch of the old house until 11:30 the night before with Randy Baxter, his farmer neighbor and drinking buddy from across the road, Jack's sluggish wakeup was assisted by two extra-strength Excedrins. Ginger and Jasmine galloped up from the woods and stood at the board fence of their summer pasture like two gin mill floosies at the mahogany bar of a seedy saloon. They were both Quarter Horse mares that would kiss Quasimoto for the right kind of treat. Ginger was a ten-year-old bay of about 14.2 hands and Jasmine a seven-year-old sorrel of about 15 hands. Neither was big by experienced horseback riders' standards, but the older Jack became, the taller the two frisky equines looked. Jack just laughed at their gustatory motives and began walking toward the barnyard, which was adjacent to the start of the one-and-a-quarter-mile bridle and running path that looped around the sixty acres of creeks, woods, pasture, and cropland.

"Hold on, ya sleazy tarts. I got some beer to run off before ya get'ny goodies. I was chairin' a symposium on politics 'n other sports late last night."

It was Saturday, the 9th of June, and the peskiest bugs had not begun to annoy the horses like they would in July, August, and September, when even facemasks and spray repellents only slightly reduced the relentless torment of black flies, greenheads, and horse flies. Ginger and Jasmine had both lost all their winter pelage, and with the warm morning sun highlighting their sleek coats and flowing manes, they were a pair of stunning girls standing side-by-side with their heads and necks extended over the black board fence. Nothing in nature stirred Jack's soul like the soft scents of an early summer morning accented by the nickering of hungry horses, the warbling of melodious song-birds, and the whispering of winter wheat.

As a former high school English teacher, Jack Sullivan provided adjunct, composition instruction at the nearby junior college whenever enrollment demands created the daytime sections that his flexible schedule allowed him to staff. Now in his late fifties, he had been divorced for nearly five years, and his two daughters were well out of college and pursuing professional careers that had yet to return the cost of their pricey undergraduate and graduate degrees from private universities. His ex-wife was remarried to a man who was much more attentive to her, decidedly less absorbed in himself, and infinitely more enhanced by money. Using his savings and severance pay as a down payment, Jack had purchased the small farm in South Central Ohio shortly after retiring from his English Department chairmanship at a large suburban high school near Columbus. Most of his friends and associates regarded the purchase as "Sullivan's Folly" because Jack had a lifelong dream of owning a farm and horses but had no experience with equines beyond his teenaged visits to riding stables where the programmed mounts followed a scripted route inexorably back to the barn. His purchase of Ginger five years before and the spirited Jasmine two years later taught him that what he knew about equine management could be written in the first paragraph of a horseman's primer. Even now, he was still in the infancy of a horse owner's development.

Loping down the rather steep declivity in the running path that ran first toward the creek before it curved around to a nearly quarter-mile of straightaway next to dense woods and brush, Jack's thoughts turned to what could be a problematic day.

At 11:00 a.m., Caitlin Cashman would be arriving with her mother, Maggie, to discuss the one-on-one writing sessions Jack had reluctantly agreed to consider for the seventeen-year-old. Randy Baxter's wife, Dorothy, a real estate agent who owned three Missouri Foxtrotters, was a friend of Maggie's, and she had pressured Jack to talk with Caitlin, who "is really bright and wants desperately to get into Rice, but she has a bit of an attitude problem since her dad's accident." As he ran, Jack was hatching some of the reasons why his working with Caitlin at the farm to refine her application essay would be laden with problems. Not the least of which would be the irritation of his being stuck one summer morning a week with a babbling high school Harriet and providing feedback to a meddling middle-aged matron who piled an extra forty-five pounds on to an amorphous body. Jack could see it already: an obstinate teen bridling at every suggestion he made on his front porch while her mama sat in the wicker rocker reading the latest Danielle Steel. They'd be driving the three miles from Clydesboro, the town of about eight thousand guileless souls whose idea of cultural broadening was to attend three, not two, country and western performances a month at the Colonial, the former movie theater converted into the town's version of the Kennedy Center for the Arts. Caitlin would be a senior in the fall at Clydesboro High School, which was something less than the Midwestern citadel of secondary school scholarship. "Rice University!" Sullivan scoffed aloud. "Walmart U'd be more like it."

Jack knew virtually nothing about Caitlin or her mother.

A Long Farewell

What little he did know was that Bob Cashman, the father and husband, had been killed in a single-car accident while driving home on State Route 50 from Cincinnati about a year and a half before. That's all Dorothy had told him other than that Maggie had done her a few favors and that Caitlin had struggled with some issues since her father's death.

By the time Jack had worked his way around the alfalfa and wheat fields, through the woods, along the corn, and back into the barnyard to complete the first lap, he had pretty much decided that he just didn't have the time to commit to improving the writing sample of a high school rube's pie-in-the-sky hopes of Rice. His decision, of course, was based upon a complete falsehood. He had more time than the pastures had manure, and there was no shortage of that. Over the course of the next three laps, he wove his tangled web, even garnishing it with the fabrication that he might take a trip to Montana that would create a disruptive hiatus to any continuity he and Caitlin might establish in their discussions. As he sprinted up the old tractor run and back into the barnyard, he was not only pleased with his beautifully detailed concoction but with his five-mile-run time, which was just under thirty-four minutes.

"Must've been the carbo loadin' from all that beer last night," he said to the horses. "I'll remember that when I run my next 10K."

He took Ginger and Jasmine's nickering for confirmation of his sage insights. In truth, all they wanted was the apple treats.

By 10:30, he had shaved and showered and donned his favorite farm uniform: a faded pair of Wrangler jeans, a time and wear-shaped baseball hat, an oft-washed Panama Jack T-shirt, and a seen-better-days pair of Georgia Farm and Ranch boots. He wolfed down a banana, some rye toast, and a tall glass of Minute Maid orange juice; by 10:45 he was seated on the front porch in one of the green plastic chairs with his feet propped on one of others, doing his best James

91

Dean pose from *Giant*. From this position he could watch the approach of any vehicle as it arrived in the driveway and navigated the nearly quarter-mile of gravel to the barnyard. While waiting, he refined how he would courteously listen to the mother's pitch on her daughter's behalf before he discreetly introduced his time limitations and the attendant reasons why he regrettably couldn't provide the help.

As much as he had wanted to avoid the meeting, when 11:15 arrived and no one had entered the driveway yet, Jack was about to give Dorothy Baxter a call to jerk her chain about a bogus appointment. Just about that time, however, a vehicle turned into the driveway from the county road, but it wasn't the rifle-equipped pickup that Jack had anticipated; it had the low profile of a car. As it made its way slowly up the lane, it resolved itself into a silver-gray BMW 750 Series sedan.

"Who-in-the-hell-is-this?" said Jack as the luxury vehicle eased into the barnyard and stopped near the open door of the tack room.

For a full thirty seconds, no one emerged, and Jack stood on the porch with his mouth slightly agape, not knowing whether to approach the car or remain where he was. Suddenly, both passenger- and driver-side doors opened, and two women who looked like sisters from a distance began walking toward the porch. Both were dressed in designer jeans, brown loafers, and form-fitting sleeveless tops. Each was wearing sunglasses and seemed to be about 5'9" and maybe 135 pounds, with legs that looked like they started at the armpits.

"Good morning!" exclaimed the driver. "Are you Mr. Sullivan?"

"Uh...yeah. I'm Jack Sullivan."

"I'm sorry we're late. It's my fault. I was held up in a meeting."

"Uh...no problem."

By this time the driver and the younger woman with her

were standing on the grass in front of the porch, looking up at Jack.

"I'm Maggie Cashman, and this is my daughter, Caitlin. I hope we haven't inconvenienced you."

"Oh...no. Please, come on up."

Once on the porch, Caitlin spoke for the first time.

"You have a beautiful place here, Mr. Sullivan. I'm sure you enjoy it immensely."

"Well, it has its moments, but the work can be a bit overwhelming at times."

"I certainly admire your mares. Quarters?"

"Why, yes. They are. Are you familiar with horses?"

"A bit."

Maggie said nothing but smiled approvingly at her daughter.

"Well, maybe I can introduce you to them before you leave."

"I'd like that very much."

"Listen, I've forgotten my manners. Can I...can I get you anything to drink? I have iced tea, soda, both diet and regular, and, of course, bottled water."

"Oh, I'd love an iced tea if it's not too much trouble," said Maggie.

"And how about you Caitlin? Anything?"

"A bottled water will be fine, thank you."

"I'll be right back."

Jack practically ran in to the kitchen, but when he got there, he didn't know what to use for the iced tea. He finally decided on some crystal glasses his late mother had given him but he'd never used. The problem was that they were in a box under the sink and very dusty. While washing the glasses for himself and Maggie, he yelled out from the kitchen, "Would you like something to eat?" No response.

That was really smooth, he thought.

He found a half box of reduced-fat Triscuits and dumped them into a mixing bowl, and then he took the drinks and the snacks through the television and living rooms and out to the porch.

"Sorry I don't have more on hand. Randy and I killed... uh, consumed most of my better snacks here on the porch last night."

"These are just fine. Please, sit down, Mr. Sullivan," said the very composed Maggie Cashman.

Suddenly, Jack felt like a ten-year-old visitor in his own house. He knew he needed to calm himself quickly and establish some credibility, if not some aplomb.

"Tell me, Mr. Sullivan," Maggie began, "do your beautiful surroundings inspire you to any creative writing?"

"Jack, please."

Maggie acquiesced with a nod and sipped on her iced tea.

"Yes. I've dabbled a bit with a novel and some short stories, but I do it only for my own entertainment. They're more flights of fancy than literature, I'm afraid."

He'd no sooner said the last word than he suspected that he'd just failed the first test. But why did he care? He had no interest in these two anyway.

"Pardon me, Mr. Sullivan," Caitlin interjected, "but isn't writing your specialty? I mean, don't you see yourself as quite skilled, both as a student and teacher of writing?"

"Well, yes, Caitlin. But I find my own work too familiar and provincial to be very profound to me, and, as such, I suspect that it wouldn't be very compelling for others."

Caitlin cast a furtive glance at her mother and then continued. "But how do you inspire confidence in your student writers if you have doubts about yourself?"

Damn! Jack thought. *Who's conducting this interview? And what happened to that fat mother and her pigheaded daughter?* Jack knew he had to shift into a more assertive demeanor, if for no other reason that to defend his skills. He resented being baited by a seventeen-year-old, in spite of the fact that she was obviously more than just bright. Mama not only had money, but she was a beautiful, mid-to-late-forties sophisticate who was clearly enjoying the performance of her daughter-clone who was playing devil's advocate with a prospective tutor. If the meeting had been a boxing match, he'd have been on the ropes for the first three rounds.

Not taking the bait entirely, Jack recovered somewhat, answering, "I don't regard myself as a personal cheerleader or a confidence coach, Caitlin. In fact, my *modus operandi* is that of a rather implacable and demanding instructor of crisp, cogent, and cohesive writing. I'm quite passionate about what I try to teach, but if your mother's hoping for a confidence builder from an old curmudgeon like me, I'm most definitely the wrong guy."

Jack feared almost instantly that he had exceeded his boundary and expected a lightning rejoinder from Maggie, but Caitlin returned his volley with equal verve.

"My mother has nothing to do with this, Mr. Sullivan, except to pay your wages if we reach an agreement. And I have only one interest, and that's the very practical use of your skills to gain admission to Rice."

Without compromising her treatise, Caitlin's tone had changed from the rather supercilious to the very busi- nesslike. Jack glimpsed at Maggie, who seemed totally dis- passionate about the exchange.

"In that case, Caitlin, here's a thumbnail rendering of my resume. I hold a B.A. in English from Xavier University, where I was steeped in British, American, and world litera- ture and had to pass a rigorous two-day comprehensive examination in order to graduate. I also hold an M.A. in English from Miami University, and my thesis addressed the social reforms effected by Charles Dickens in nineteenth cen- tury England. I taught high school English for thirty years, the last twelve of which were at Otterbein High School, where I served as an advanced placement teacher and department head. Since retirement, I've entertained myself somewhat by teaching composition on a part-time basis at Macon Junior College."

Maggie Cashman could no longer refrain.

"You've come highly recommended, Mr. Sullivan," her formality returning. "We have every confidence in your abilities."

Jack laughed and glanced at Caitlin, who seemed a bit off-put by her mother's intervention.

"I didn't mean to appear condescending or abrasive. If I can be of any help with Caitlin's essay, I'll be delighted to work with her. I must tell you, however, that I'll have to exclude any guarantees of success from my contract if you decide to employ me. But even if you don't, please call me Jack."

Jack's tone was intended to be jocular and conciliatory, and it was supported by a reassuring grin.

"I know a little about contracts, Jack. And if this works out, perhaps we can just rely on a cordial handshake."

In spite of her striking good looks and urbane bearing, Maggie manifested a natural warmth that was underscored by a come-hither smile. Jack was a goner.

"You bet!"

Maggie rose from her chair, and said to Caitlin, "Honey, I hate to cut this discussion short, but I really need to get back to the office and organize my notes from this morning's meeting while they're still fresh in my mind."

Jack's curiosity had reached its bursting point.

"What kind of work do you do, Maggie?"

Caitlin seemed to smile at Jack sardonically, as her mother replied.

"I'm an attorney, Jack, specializing in contract negotiations."

Although she divulged the information almost apologetically, Jack felt like the prince of fools. For some reason, he simply hadn't seen that coming.

"Oh!"

He had become the ten-year-old again, but he tried to recover.

"Well, Caitlin. If you think I can help you any, let me know."

"I will, and thank you, Mr. Sullivan. I hope I didn't appear disrespectful."

"Not at all. I enjoyed the exchange. Caitlin, please pardon my asking, but have you taken your SAT's yet?"

"Yes. I took them in May."

Offering the answer to what she quickly divined that Jack wanted to know, she provided her results.

"I scored a 2,210. 710 on the math, 760 on the reading, and 740 on the writing."

"Congratulations! That's very impressive."

Caitlin was too well grounded to be blinded by her own brilliance.

"Perhaps, but since most of the other Rice applicants will be posting similar scores, I'll need to nail the essay."

"Indeed. You will."

On the way to the car, Jack, Maggie, and Caitlin stopped to see Ginger and Jasmine. Caitlin fed them some apple-flavored biscuits from a bag, and they responded enthusiastically to her requests for kisses. Often able to insinuate themselves into a visitor's favor, the mares played the equine charmers on this beautiful day. Jack looked at Maggie, who suddenly showed signs of sadness in spite of her smile. At the car, Jack told Maggie and Caitlin to let him know what they wanted to do, and they both thanked him again for his time. Maggie turned the BMW around in the barnyard and headed for the driveway. Jack walked back to the steps of the porch, feeling like he had blown the interview, but the car stopped and Maggie got out with the engine still running. She walked quickly over to Jack and extended her hand.

"Jack, would $75.00 an hour meet your expectations?"

Jack just laughed and took her hand and shook it gently.

"That's way too much."

"Not if you get that girl into Rice."

"Maggie, I can't guaran…"

"I know. I know. But I can tell that she's sold on you and that's what's important to me."

"Then I'll take the job. We can start next Saturday morning at ten for two hours a session, if that works for her and you."

"That'll be fine, I'm sure."

"Maggie, I'm more than a little curious. Caitlin didn't seem too impressed with me. What 'sold' her?"

"I'd only be guessing, but I'd say that to some extent it was your T-shirt, boots, and jeans, and, of course, that dashing ball hat, but it was mostly your beautiful girls over there."

She smiled and winked at him impishly.

"And not me irrepressible oyrish charm?"

"Yeah. That too, I guess."

Maggie beamed and blushed a little. What she didn't say was that it was that Irish charm that sold her on Jack, and not for just as a tutor for her talented but troubled daughter.

"She'll be here next Saturday."

"By the way, how does she rank in her class?"

"Right now, she's in a dead-heat tie with two boys for next year's valedictorian. And she's likely to retain her first singles spot on the tennis team in the fall."

"You must be very proud."

"And very worried. I'll tell you more when I get the chance."

"Does she have a laptop?"

"Oh, yeah."

"Tell'er to bring it."

"See ya!"

Over the next week Jack tried brainstorming some ideas for topic suggestions that would not only avoid the mundane but provide the salient discussion the girl would need to raise her Rice application above the logjam of the other eminently qualified candidates. Caitlin's insights were most accurate: her lofty SAT scores would be about the norm for most of the serious applicants. A phone call to Dorothy Baxter revealed more than the sketchy information she had previously provided about Maggie and Caitlin.

"How come you didn't tell me Maggie was an attorney?"

"I thought I told you that."

"Yeah, you thought you told me that. You told me nuttin, sister."

"I told you she had done me a few favors."

"Legal?"

"We got to know each other at the health club, and she offered to help me *pro bono* regarding some inheritance disputes with my siblings. That was about five or six months after Bob's accident. Over lunch one day after an aerobics class, she poured her heart out a little about Caitlin's difficulty with Bob's death."

"What kind of work did Bob do?"

"You don't know much, do ya?"

"I'm not one of you local yokels, ya know. I don't know everyone's history."

"Oh, I know, you're just so damned uptown. Dr. Robert Cashman was an oncologist in Cincinnati. He had his own clinic. He was coming home late from the city a year ago last January when he hit some black ice. He rolled his Jaguar about three times. He was wearing a belt, but he was dead at the scene."

"Were he and Caitlin close?"

"Very. The Cashmans have a gorgeous home out off Wildcat Road with a pool and a tennis court. Bob and Caitlin played tennis together whenever the two had free time. Bob played for Ohio State."

"You didn't bother to tell me they had money out the gazzu."

"Would you have helped Caitlin if I had?"

"Do you think I'm wagin' some kind of lifelong class war?"

"Would you have helped her?"

"Probably not, but she's likely well beyond any help I can giv'er anyway. I haven't thought of anything meaningful for her essay."

"Is that your job?"

"Well, no, but she's got to find something that really jumps off the page for a topic. I feel like I've at least got to giv'er some food for thought."

"Look, Professor. You gonna take the credit if she gets in?"

"Hell, no!"

"Then you're not to blame if she doesn't. Just be honest with her."

"You need to hang out a shingle. Any charge for this advice?"

"Yeah. Muck my stalls."

"Bye."

The following Saturday, Jack arose early and finished an abbreviated run by 8:30. He'd even curtailed his beer drinking on the porch with Randy the night before, hoping to be as sharp as possible in the morning. His temperance didn't escape Baxter's attention, and once or twice the grain farmer remarked upon the English teacher's questionable fervor.

"You're fallin' behind, buddy. I can only carry ya so long."

"Since when do you need me to kill any part of a twelve pack?"

"Since never, but I think that little girl's got ya by the shorthairs."

"Naah. Well...maybe a little. She'll be a challenge to challenge."

"What'er ya gonna start with?"

"Brainstorm some, I guess. Whatya know about her mother?"

Baxter belched and then laughed derisively.

"Ya noticed her too, huh."

"A little, maybe."

" 'A little, maybe.' You'd damned well like to be ridin' in her saddle. I won't say she's completely outta your league, but her sophistication would intimidate me some."

"Are you shittin' me? Ginger's sophistication would intimidate you some."

"My point, exactly. But you'd better take care not to get your hopes up with that lady."

Baxter, the beer-bottle philosopher, was probably right again.

Jack was showered and shaved by 9:30, so he spent the next half hour arranging and rearranging the front porch tables and chairs. He'd made some lemonade from concentrate and opened some boxes of bagels and doughnuts he'd bought. He wasn't sure whether his anxiety was greater in regard to his skills or being alone with Caitlin. Maggie didn't seem at all concerned, but he'd need a while to get comfortable with this arrangement.

Right at ten o'clock, a yellow Jeep Wrangler turned off the county road and barreled up the lane, almost going airborne over one or two humps. Stopping by the tack room, Caitlin jumped out in a T-shirt, boot-cut jeans, and a pair of Ariat boots. She carried a laptop in a shoulder bag and a Starbucks in her hand.

"Morning!" she hollered from the barnyard.

"Good morning," Sullivan replied. "You're thirty seconds late."

"I can take that lane faster if ya want."

"I'm just kidding, really."

Once on the porch Caitlin engaged Jack in a brief discussion about Ginger and Jasmine and expressed her keen interest in riding them. She also mentioned the personal lessons she was taking with tennis pros in Chillicothe on Wednesdays and Fridays. After some further horse talk, they settled in for the day's work.

"Did you get the voice-mail message I left you about the writing samples?"

John Hagan

"Yeah, I brought copies of two essays I wrote last semester in my A. P. class."

Caitlin pulled them out of her computer bag and handed them to Jack. While Jack sat on an old porch swing and read, Caitlin sat in the wicker rocker and munched on one of the bagels her host had set on a small table.

"I'd like to go see the girls while you read the second one, if you don't mind."

"Be my guest. Betcha can't resist givin' 'em the treats from the bag by the fence."

"I won't take that bet."

While Caitlin talked to the horses, Jack read the second essay, the topic of which was stem cell therapy. He was most impressed with the profundity of her viewpoint and her balance on the issue. There was nothing of the puerile in her analysis, and her conclusion was supported with clearly stated evidence, but she was a bit verbose in some sections and drifted into the *ad hominem* and *ad populum* fallacies in others. By the time Caitlin returned to the porch, Jack had finished both essays and written some notes in the margins for himself.

"Well, what do you think?"

"Good work, but..."

"But?"

Caitlin had clearly expected a review of both essays in superlative terms, having received an A on one and an A+ on the other.

"Well, let's talk about some of the notes I took."

Over the next forty-five minutes, Jack expanded on his notes and offered Caitlin advice that he detected she'd not previously heard. He was struck by some of her comments, however, that told to him he'd greatly underestimated the quality of instruction at Clydesboro High School.

Showing some of her petulance, Caitlin asked almost perfunctorily, "What's next?"

"I'd say we brainstorm for your Rice essay topic."

"Any ideas?"

"That's your department. Have you thought about it at all?"

"Well, yes. But all my topics seem so overworked."

"Give me a few."

"You have one in your hand. I've also thought about the abortion and immigration issues. I have some very strong views about them, but they don't seem..."

"I'd agree. How about something more personal, more specifically gritty?"

Caitlin didn't respond at first, but then began.

"Well...there is something I'd like to talk about, but I don't think it has much of a broad-based impact."

Jack didn't answer. He just nodded.

"I'd like to discuss my dad's death and my reaction to it, but I dunno."

"I can't get inside the heads of the Rice readers, but I think it has merit."

"Really!"

"Go with it. Listen, you've got thirty minutes of your two hours left. Put that laptop to work and get started."

"I couldn't write about that here."

"Get started while I put the horses in their stalls to keep the flies off 'em. Inspire and sustain yourself with another bagel."

Caitlin scrunched her face but said, "Okay."

Jack took the horses down to the barn, but he didn't stall them up. Instead, he brushed and combed them, and then saddled them up. Caitlin worked for about thirty-five minutes before walking down to the barnyard with her laptop.

"Mr. Sullivan."

Jack responded by walking out of the barn with the saddled Ginger, smiling.

"Got time for a ride?"

"All day!"

"Here, you hold Ginger while I get Jasmine."

103

When he returned with Jasmine, Caitlin held both horses while Jack sat on a hay bale and read what she had written on the laptop. He put it down without editorial comment and walked to Caitlin and the horses.

"Finish it this week, and we'll talk about it next Saturday. You can ride Ginger, and I'll ride Jasmine."

"Can't I ride Jasmine? I love sorrels."

"I don't think so. Jasmine can be a handful, even for me, and I know her spook issues."

Caitlin looked at Jack in a way that told him if she didn't get her way, he'd quickly become *persona non grata*. He also figured she had perfected the look.

"Really, Mr. Sullivan, I'll be okay."

Against his better judgment, Jack agreed.

"All right, but I'm not at all comfortable with this."

They started down the hill of the bridle path that Jack had run earlier that morning. After they made the curve at the bottom, Caitlin came from behind Jack and rode up beside him.

"Do you suppose we could pick it up a little?"

"Well, maybe, a bit."

With that, Caitlin gave Jasmine a kick, and together horse and rider galloped down the straightaway of the bridle path with clods of dirt and sod flying.

"Oh, shit!" shot Jack as he picked it up with Ginger.

When she reached the end of the straightaway, Caitlin waited for Jack, who was coming up quickly.

"I just lov'er, Jack! Uh...Mr. Sullivan."

"You just scared the bejeebers outta me! Now, slow down and don't do that to me again."

For the rest of the ride, Jack and Caitlin let their hair down a little, and in subtle ways the girl made references to her father's death and implied that she was carrying considerable resentment for her mother. She also revealed that she could manage Jasmine as casually as she could chew gum. After they finished the ride and brushed and cooled the horses, Jack and Caitlin walked to the Wrangler.

"You be careful driving, Caitlin. I'll see you next Saturday, and we'll look at your draft."

"I'll work on it next week. Ten o'clock again?"

"Yep. And Caitlin, you can call me Jack."

"Really! Thanks, Jack."

Jack spent the rest of the day cleaning stalls and replacing some damaged siding on the back of the barn. He was in and out of thoughts about Caitlin and Maggie. He could only guess why Caitlin would be so resentful of her mother, and the guess wasn't kind to Maggie.

After his dinner of a can of Campbell's soup and a turkey, tomato, and lettuce sandwich, Jack sat on the front porch and worked on a short story with an Eagle pencil and a ringed notebook. Around 7:15, a car turned into the driveway and eased its way up from the road.

"I'll be damned!"

He could see from a distance that it was Maggie Cashman's BMW. It approached very slowly and seemed to take forever to pull into the barnyard. When the driver's side door opened, Jack saw two very toned and shapely legs extend before Maggie emerged in a pair of shorts and sandals coordinating perfectly with a sleeveless blouse that exposed two equally toned and shapely arms. She carried a bottle of wine in one hand and two glasses in another.

"Hi!"

"Hi, yourself," Jack yelled from the porch. "You lost?"

"Could be. I'm lookin' for a happy Irishman to lift my spirits."

"C'mon up. I'll see if I can find ya one."

Maggie was coming up, invited or not. She was just bold enough without being overbearing or suffocating. For the first time since Jack had met her, she also seemed a little vulnerable. She set the wine and glasses on the table.

"Vino?"

"Don't mind if I do."

She had already popped the cork, so Jack poured them each a husky glass of white zinfandel. He motioned Maggie to a chair, and she plopped down and crossed her gorgeous legs. She said nothing for so long that Jack finally broke the silence with the timeless classic.

"So, what's a nice girl like you doin' in a place like this? On a Saturday night?"

"Well, first of all, my daughter doesn't think I'm a very nice girl. And second of all, what's the matter with a place like this? I think it's Heaven-on-Earth."

"If you're tryin' to seduce me, your technique is working."

Maggie threw her head back and laughed.

"If I weren't so preoccupied, I'd go for it right now, but I need to talk to you about Caitlin first."

"Now you've got me caught between desire and duty."

"Did she tell you why she's so angry with me?"

"Only obliquely. She never got right to the point, and I didn't press her."

"It has to do with her dad's death."

"Gathered that."

"She and Bob were very close. So close, in fact, I was on the periphery of full-blown jealousy at times."

"Really!"

"Well, maybe not jealousy exactly, just wounded pride because I felt left out. They didn't leave me out willfully, just naturally. Whenever I tried to enter their world, I felt like they were accommodating me rather than engaging me. And at times, when my law work became oppressive, I'd take umbrage to their bonding when I needed their attentions."

"And?"

"And, I'd start little skirmishes with Bob over something inconsequential, and Caitlin would notice. Well, one morning, a year ago last January, Bob told me he was taking Caitlin to Chillicothe that night for some indoor tennis, and I went off. He went out in a huff, and Caitlin heard and saw the whole thing. That evening we got the call from the State

Patrol. She thinks I'm to blame, and she hasn't forgiven me."

"Has she told you that?"

"Never. I just know."

After a pensive pause, Jack continued, "I see."

"You do?"

"Yep. Your only mistake here is that you're beginning to think she's right, and your only fault, if it can be called one, was in loving and needing them so much you couldn't bear what you thought was their indifference."

"Are you charging me for this?"

"Damned right, and it's gonna cost you a lot more than seventy-five bucks an hour."

"And I thought we lawyers were supposed to be the only shysters."

Jack laughed.

"No, we snake oil salesmen are everywhere, but you're right about one thing. Caitlin has a penchant for the *ad hominem*. I've seen it in her essays."

Maggie put down her wine glass, stood up, and walked over to Jack. She took his glass and then sat on his lap.

"You know, Mr. Sullivan, you're about the most refreshing sonofabitch I've met in a long time."

"What part of my charm first stole your heart?"

"Not entirely sure, but your toe-to-toe with Caitlin last week made me see a feisty side mixed with a certain panache."

"Panache, you're calling me 'panache.' I've never been so insulted. In fact, I..."

She put her hand over his mouth, and when she withdrew it, she kissed him lightly at first and then with a vigor that suggested a woman who hadn't been loved for quite a while. They finished the wine, and about three hours later, Maggie put her sandals on to leave.

"Please help her with that essay."

"You know I'll do my best."

"How long do you think you'll need to get it written?"

"I don't think it'll take very long once she refines her topic and sharpens her thesis."

"Is she leaning in any direction?"

"Yep."

"Bob's death?"

"Yep. Want me to steer her away from it?"

"Absolutely not! Maybe it'd be cathartic for her to write about it."

"Hey, 'cathartic' is a Shakespeare teacher's word. You can't use that."

"I just used you, didn't I?"

"So, you did, you dirty hussy."

"Gotta go. It's eleven o'clock and my daughter doesn't know where her mother is."

"I didn't know she could ride so well."

"Oh, didn't she tell you? She started riding in 4-H when she was six."

"Geez!"

"I'll call ya."

Jack spent the next week occupied with farm chores, but his thoughts were dominated by the allure of his new employer and the anger of his current student. How could he reconcile his affection for Maggie with his obligation to Caitlin? No answers he reached seemed to be fair to both. Even running the bridle trail, which often crystallized his thinking, failed to produce a satisfying resolution to his dilemma.

The next Saturday, Caitlin arrived right on time, but she brought her own alfalfa treats for the horses, and she went first to the fence for a kisses-and-treats visit while Jack was left to cool his heels on the porch.

"You know, you could at least let me read your work while you play with those nags."

"I'm coming. I just wanted to say 'Hi!' to my girls."

"Well, bring me the essay first."

"I'm coming."

She left the horses and ambled across the yard and up on to the porch.

"No food?"

"There's some fresh orange juice in the fridge and some bagels on the hutch, but your server has the day off."

She handed him the hard copy of her essay and marched boldly into the house to feed her insatiable teenage appetite. Jack began reading with his pencil-in-mouth technique and made his nearly compulsive notes in the margins. When Caitlin returned to the porch, she plopped in the wicker rocker and worked on her bagel and juice. She said nothing until Jack put down the essay.

"Okay. What's the verdict?"

"I like it. It needs some work, but I like it. It has an emotional appeal but avoids the maudlin. It says what you feel without the invective. Your indictments are mild and tempered."

As expected, Caitlin's personal essay explored the gamut of her emotions in the aftermath of her father's sudden death. She explained and justified the reasons why reconciliation with her mother would be unlikely, and she maintained that while her resentment was not entirely rational, it was predictable and natural, given her affections for her father. She established her relationship with her father that made her mother's sniping seem more egregious and contributory to his accident. She claimed no infallibility in the matter, only observations. Her discussion was thorough but not verbose, fact-based but not tedious, and candid but not brutal.

"So, you think it's ready?"

"Hardly. Read my marginal notes regarding some organizational issues, word choices, and some *non sequitur* and *post hoc* fallacies."

Jack handed her the copy, and Caitlin studied the notes for about five minutes before looking up with a heavy sigh.

"So it's back to the drawing board."

"Not entirely, but you do need to make some changes. I'm headin' down to the barn. Use the next hour or so and my notes to make some adjustments in your laptop. There's cold meat and fresh bread in the house if you wanna make yourself a sandwich."

Jack went down to the barn and began cleaning and organizing the tack room in what was the quintessential exercise in futility. Caitlin sat on the porch and began the suggested revisions and improvements. About an hour later, she brought the laptop down to the barnyard and dropped it on the passenger seat of the Wrangler.

"Finished?"

"For today, at least."

"Wanna go for a ride?"

"Yep."

They saddled the horses, and then Caitlin, of course, hopped on Jasmine. When they reached the bottom of the hill again, Caitlin looked at Jack, and he just smiled and nodded. With that, she gave the very fresh Jasmine a slight nudge and off they went with turf flying. When Jack finally caught up, he and Caitlin settled into a side-by-side walk around the farm. Caitlin broached the subject.

"Jack, you said something on the porch that kind of surprised me."

"What?"

"You said that my indictments were mild. I don't think I'm indicting anyone exactly. I'm just characterizing a family situation."

"Hey, don't whine to me about what you've described. If it's a tell-it-like-it-was essay, then have the courage to handle the carnage that goes with it."

"Carnage, what carnage?"

"You know what I mean."

"Jack, what my dad and I had was great. We couldn't help that my mom felt left out. That was her impression, and because she couldn't accept it, she'd lash out at Dad. Just

110

like that morning before he left, and..."

"Let me tell ya something. For years, I indulged myself in my teaching and running, and I just assumed that my wife could find fulfillment and companionship with our girls. I gave little or no thought to her needs or feelings. One day, after the girls were gone, she just left me, and then and only then did I realize how neglectful I had been and how much I needed her. Now, I know my situation wasn't entirely the same as the yours, but I daresay that while it may take a long time, you'll eventually see what your cozy little relationship with your dad was doing to your mom."

"That's bullshit! It wasn't any 'cozy little relationship.' You'd never understand how much I loved my dad."

Caitlin gave Jasmine a kick and raced off. By the time Jack finally walked Ginger back into the barnyard, Caitlin had the tack off of Jasmine and was brushing her down. After she turned Jasmine out, she went to the Wrangler.

"Will you look at my final draft next week? I'd like to have everything ready for an early-action application as soon as possible."

"You know I will. Caitlin, I'm sorry if I overstepped my role."

"Forget it!"

The following Wednesday Jack took a call from Dorothy Baxter. He could tell from the caller I.D. that it was his neighbor.

"Start talkin'."

"Heard your student came home pretty upset Saturday."

"And how'd you hear that?"

"Little bird, maybe."

"Well, did that little bird say if I was fired?"

"I think that little bird thinks you've got your hands full, but she said she has every confidence in you."

"To which you said?"

"To which I said that with the possible exception of my husband you're the biggest pain in the ass I've ever met."

"How can I thank you?"

"Muck my stalls."

"Bye."

The next Saturday, right at ten, the yellow Jeep turned into the lane but progressed much more slowly than at its typical Mach 3 speeds. Once at the barn, two "wranglers" got out of the Wrangler and headed toward the porch. Each was dressed in blue jeans, riding boots, and a denim shirt. The younger of the two carried a manila envelope that she handed up to Jack, who was standing on the top porch step.

"We were wondering if we could borrow a couple of your mounts, pardner," said Caitlin.

Maggie stood by like a hopeful child waiting for Santa's answer.

"I think that could be arranged. They just happen to be stalled up already."

Jack put the envelope on the table and walked with them to the barn. Maggie just smiled at him and shrugged her shoulders. After helping with the tack, Jack walked with Maggie and Ginger, and they followed Caitlin and Jasmine out of the barn.

Jack whispered, "Have you read her essay?"

"Nope."

Caitlin took the lead down the hill, but at the bottom, she and Maggie just walked the horses side-by-side down the straightaway. *Oh boy,* thought Jack as he watched from the board fence near the barn.

Once on the porch, Jack began reading Caitlin's Rice application essay. It was completely devoid of the errors he had pointed out in the draft, and it was skillfully and tastefully written. It just wasn't the essay he had read the previous Saturday. In the new one, Caitlin delineated the struggle she had had with her father's passing and her reaction to her mother in the aftermath. The pivotal point was that it had taken her father's death for her to recognize her mother's pain and her own selfishness. Her thesis, of course, was that

112

a catastrophic event shouldn't have to be the wake-up call to a self-absorbed teen. Avoiding superfluous sentimentality, she established her epiphany in a graphic, candid, and introspective way. It was brilliant.

"And all without my splendid help, dammit!"

About forty minutes after Jack finished reading the essay, Caitlin and Maggie rode up the tractor run and into the barnyard. When Jack started down the steps, Maggie waved him off.

"We'll handle this, Jack."

After brushing the horses and turning them out, Caitlin walked to the porch while Maggie got into the Wrangler. Jack handed Caitlin the envelope.

"Any corrections?"

"None! If that's not good enough for Rice, I wouldn't know what would be."

"Well, I hope it is, but even if it's not, I've got something that's so much better than Rice. My mom."

"When didya realize that?"

"Writing this painful essay Monday and Tuesday, and riding those gorgeous girls today."

"Good luck, Caitlin Cashman!"

"Thank you, Jack Sullivan!"

As Caitlin headed for the car, Maggie got out and walked up to the porch.

"I almost forgot to give you this."

She handed him a personal check.

"Maggie, I really have been paid already."

"I'll be seeing you later, mister. I'm taking you to dinner at Mecklenburg Gardens. Can you be ready by six?"

"I'll have the dirt outta my ears and the manure offa my boots."

Jack watched from the porch as the Wrangler headed down the lane.

"I wonder what those damned horses told Caitlin."

The Motion Picture

On a Montana road that marks the general divide between the Gallatin and Absaroka Mountains, a traveler, accompanied only by his Border Collie, drove his Chevy Blazer through the region officially and romantically known as Paradise Valley. The traveler, an Ohio man in his mid-fifties, had retired three years before after a thirty-year career as a high school English teacher. The road, U.S. Highway 89, is a ribbon of asphalt that gift wraps spectacular views for the motorist who travels the fifty-one miles southward from Livingston to Gardner and follows the Yellowstone River and a magnificent stretch of the Rockies. The drive took the man past numerous signs bearing bucolic names such as Mill Creek Road, Yankee Jim's Canyon, and Brogan's Sand and Gravel. He could easily have been seduced by the sylvan sirens of quaint sounding places like Emigrant, Chico, and Pray, villages that are as obscure and low-profile as to being principally represented by rough and seedy saloons to those that are as upscale and high-end as to being characterized by opulent and trendy resorts. The region abounds with marvelous opportunities and perfect venues for horseback riding, game hunting, back packing, road running, and the intoxicant of many a Midwestern sojourner, fly-fishing.

114

A Long Farewell

While sterling vistas for horseback riding were most appealing to the traveler, Sean Fallon, of paramount interest to him was the valley's purported proximity to many of the scenes from a motion picture that for some reason had begun to fixate and consume him. Fallon was so captivated by *The Horse Whisperer* that he had interrupted a post-retirement position as an adjunct, composition instructor to follow his fanciful notions to an outcome that would surely resolve itself in predictable disappointment. Did he expect a seductive Kristin Scott Thomas stretched on a Gallatin Mountain rock, awaiting his amorous attentions, or a cele-bratory Robert Redford perched on a Livingston Bar and Grille stool, hoping to stand him to a stout? While the two phenomena were equally absurd, they were as plausible as any explanation he could concoct for this quixotic trek across country. Although storylines or characters often enchant beholders of compelling films, Fallon had become so consumed by Redford's masterful direction of Nicholas Evans's novel that he had practically memorized the dia-logue.

During the drive from Ohio, Fallon's mind was often flooded with thoughts of *The Horse Whisperer* and the itiner-ary followed by Kristin Scott Thomas's character, Annie Maclean. In addition to his touristy visits to Mount Rushmore, Devil's Tower, and Pompey's Pillar, he took the 212-Broadus exit from I-90 to the Little Big Horn Battleground and Memorial. Making the stop purely to re-create the visit paid by Annie Maclean, Fallon found that the historical site was, indeed, open, but on that warm and early October afternoon, he seemingly had the place to himself. Brandie, his Border Collie, had to wait in the car, but as he walked from the parking lot up the pathway to the tombstone monolith overlooking the battlefield, the soft wind sporadi-cally waved the grasses and eerily teased his ears. He was unexpectedly overcome by the solemnity of the scene of a massacre that had occurred in 1876. When he reached the mass grave, he looked out over the undulating topography that rose from the tree-lined Little Big Horn River to his own position, and he pondered the many white markers where at least one of George Armstrong Custer's troopers had fallen. The spot where Custer's body had lain was, of course, conspicuously marked in black, but nearly every slain trooper was duly noted. Standing alone with his hands on what he thought was the same iron fence grasped by the anguished Annie Maclean, he could almost hear the cacophony and imagine the melee as Custer and his men slew their horses for breastplates and died to a man at this last significant victory of a noble plains people trying desperately to preserve their time-honored way of life. He wondered why Redford had not developed the scene at greater length, but he realized that succinct as it was, it had drawn him to this powerful place.

On a late Sunday afternoon, Fallon took the exit from I-90 to U.S. 89 and entered the area just south of Livingston, Montana. Thinking that most anyone could provide copious details regarding the ranch scenes from *The Horse Whisperer,* he was surprised that no one in gas stations, convenience stores, or motel offices could or would reveal anything. They were either the most uninformed people he'd ever met or the most reticent.

Pretty much sight unseen, Fallon had booked for a week one of the cabins provided by the Dome Mountain Ranch, a 5,000-acre spread that catered primarily to fly fishermen, game hunters, and horseback riders. Owned by a media mogul in the East, it was operated by a husband and wife management team that was ably assisted by a gorgeous female wrangler and a handsome thirties-something fishing guide. Fallon reached the main lodge on U.S. 89 about thirty miles south of Livingston around 6:30 p.m. and was greeted by the very gracious managers, Renee and T. J. Decker, who showed him to his cabin and made him feel most welcome but shied from questions regarding ranch scenes from *The*

A Long Farewell

Horse Whisperer.

For the morning of his first full day at Dome Mountain, Renee had scheduled Fallon for a two-hour horseback ride in the Absaroka Mountains. His guide, a thirty-two-year-old wrangler named Jessie, was a luscious 5'9" strawberry blonde who contributed immensely to the breath-taking scenery indigenous to the area. She was from Gillette, Wyoming, and had majored in Equestrian Studies at the University of Idaho, where she had earned both her bachelor's and master's degrees. She would meet Fallon at the horse barn down the road from his cabin at 9:30 and introduce him to his mount, the nine-year-old chestnut gelding Baxter. To say that Fallon was somewhat delighted by the allure of his guide would be like saying that General Washington was mildly pleased by the arrival of General Lafayette. Although the canopy was a cerulean blue with a sprinkling of cirrus clouds, the temperature was still only in the high 50's, and Jessie was dressed in a weathered pair of Ariat boots, a tight pair of Lee jeans, and a clingy T-shirt under a long-sleeved flannel shirt, opened in the front and tied in a knot at her very small waist.

"Mornin'," she said over her shoulder as Fallon approached her from his Blazer.

"Good morning! I'm Sean Fallon. I'm scheduled for a two-hour..."

"I know. I'm just givin' the horses a little grain so they won't be tryin' to eat during our ride."

She had yet to turn around because she was hoof-picking her own horse's left front foot. Fallon took full advantage of the opportunity to leer unabashedly at the curvaceous buns that were nearly bursting the seams of her jeans.

Fallon had attempted to cowboy-up as much as possible without looking too much the fool. He pumped iron regularly, so he believed he looked pretty good in a black T-shirt with a raffish logo from Kevin Barry's Irish Bar. He had brought two pairs of well-washed, boot-cut Wranglers with him on the trip, and he had donned a pair for the ride. Shod in his Justin cowboy boots and topped in his university ball hat, he figured he looked like a young stud.

When Jessie finally turned and appraised him, her obvious indifference brought him to ground like a meteor tearing into the Earth's surface.

"M'name's Jessie. Ya might wanna grab a long-sleeve if ya have one in the car. It'll be a little chilly for a while."

"Oh, I'll be fine. Thanks."

"Suit yourself."

She was right, of course. His teeth were almost chattering already.

The ride itself was everything he hoped it would be. Jessie was enormously knowledgeable about the region, and she shared mountain anecdotes and perilous experiences as she alerted him to trail hazards and animal dangers. Her horse, Marigold, was a big buckskin mare that looked like a handful, but Jessie managed her with an impressive nonchalance while maintaining a monologue, punctuated occasionally with personal questions for Fallon. For his part, Fallon was more than content to follow behind and hanker after Jessie, who, by halfway through the ride, had shucked the flannel shirt and begun to soak up the warm sunshine from one of the few remaining Indian summer days.

"What brings ya to this part of Montana?"

"Would you believe my 'unbridled' passion for horseback riding in the Absaroka Mountains?"

She didn't grace the pitiful pun with so much as a smile.

"Would you believe I'm a National Security Agent on assignment in Paradise Valley? No, Mr. Fallon, I don't believe you're that passionate about horses."

"Well, first, please call me Sean. And second, if I told you why I'm here, you'd think my bread wasn't quite done."

For the first time since Fallon had met her, he heard Jessie laugh. It was a low, throaty Kathleen Turner laugh, almost out of sync with her speaking voice. Also, for the first time, she dropped back and rode beside him, which disappointed Fallon a little.

"You're a teacher, aren't ya?"

"I was."

"Fired?"

"No! Retired. Sort of."

"I'm bettin' English. High school or college?"

"Both! How'd ya guess?"

"Your language and comments pretty much gave you away."

His literary allusions to their surroundings were not, after all, beyond her ken.

"I was hopin' you'd think I was a retired bronc rider."

"Oh, yeah! Thought so right off, but when ya said, ' "This [mountain] hath a pleasant seat: the air nimbly and sweetly recommends itself," ' I kinda backed offa that. *Macbeth* isn't it?"

"Wow! You're pretty damned smart for a...what is it a..."

"An Equestrian Studies major. Listen, I cracked a 1,350 on my SAT's. I could've majored in anything. I had a partial, undergraduate scholarship and a full fellowship with stipend for my master's degree."

"I'm impressed."

"No you're not."

"Do you always get so sassy with ranch guests?"

"Didya always think the sexy coeds had the hots for ya?"

Breaking up by her pluck and candor, he chortled in false incredulity, "They didn't?"

"Listen. No matter how seductively they sat in their chairs or how low they wore their tops or their jeans, they only wanted one thing from you."

"My sinewy body?"

"A's."

"Really?"

"Really. They got 'em, didn't they?"

"Not always."

119

"Well, that's what they wanted."

"Are you sure?"

Fallon was really getting to like this girl.

"Whoa."

Jessie reined in Marigold, and Baxter stopped too.

"Trust me. I know."

She flashed him one of the most beautiful smiles he had ever seen. It exploded from exquisitely white choppers framed by naturally voluptuous lips and tanned cheeks that were accented by wisps of wind-blown hair. She quickly took the lead again and made only the most perfunctory small talk for the rest of the ride.

As she was tying the horses to the iron rail outside the stables, Jessie questioned Fallon again.

"Really, why are ya here?"

"I think I'm in love with a movie."

"Which one?"

The Horse Whisperer.

"Oh, yeah. I heard it was filmed around here."

"That's all anyone will tell me."

"People around here probably don't like nosey buzzards like you."

"Do guest, trail riders generally tip you?"

The infectious smile engulfed her face again and completely disarmed him.

"Aren't you gonna?"

He laughed in spite of himself and handed her a twenty.

"Can you give me any information?"

"Who was in it?"

"Well, Redford directed it and starred in it, and the female lead was Kristin Scott Thomas."

"Yeah...she's real classy."

"So, you are familiar with the movie."

"Are you in love with *The Horse Whisperer* or Kristin Scott Thomas?"

"She was great in *Four Weddings and a Funeral.*"

"She was damned good in *The English Patient,* too, but ya didn't answer my question."

"Didya read the book?"

"Of course, I did. Didn't everybody?"

"I liked her a lot in *Random Hearts.*"

"Never saw it."

Fallon looked at his watch and said, "Well, I'm gonna head on up to Livingston for lunch today and ask around. See if anybody'll tell me anything."

"What are ya hopin' to find?"

"I dunno for sure. Locate some of the scenes from the movie maybe. I actually found one of them on the way out here."

"Which one?"

"The Lazy J Motel. It's in Big Timber."

"Yeah, it is."

"I got the manager to take my picture in front of it."

"Your bubble's really off-center."

"Maybe, but you obviously know about the Lazy J."

"Not much."

Fallon just shook his head and smiled.

"What's with everybody?"

Jessie just looked at the ground, but when he turned to leave, she stopped him.

"Look, let me give you some names of some joints in Livingston."

She jotted some establishment names on a Dome Mountain Ranch note pad and handed them to him.

"Ya ever go to any of these?"

"Sometimes. Talk to the barmaids and servers. They might help ya, if ya tip 'em well."

"Thanks!"

"Thanks for the twenty, Sean Fallon!"

"Thanks for the ride, Jessie...?"

"Kearney, Jessica Lynn Kearney. But I'm not supposed to give ya my full name."

121

"You're Irish!"

"Yep."

"I'll be damned!"

That day for lunch he checked out Murray's Café. He ordered a fish sandwich, some fries, and a beer. He tried to make some inroads with the waitress, but she was much too busy at noon to encourage conversation. He drove back to the cabin and worked on some poetry in his notebook for a few hours and then took Brandie for a rather taxing walk in the mountains before turning in. He was planning a really long run in the morning.

On Tuesday morning, he arose around 6:45 and pushed in one of the bananas he had picked up in a convenience store on 89 near Emigrant. He finished his daily ritual, 300 crunches, and laced up his aging Reeboks. He let Brandie out for her morning constitutional, and by 7:30 he was walking from his cabin past the main lodge and was surprised to find a swirl of activity and cluster of people in the lobby. They were obviously preparing to head somewhere in three identical vans parked in front of the porch, but from what Fallon could see, they didn't have the look of fly fishermen.

Like the previous morning, the temperature was still only in the high 50's, so Fallon wore some baggy cotton shorts and a long-sleeved T-shirt. He first headed south on 89 in the direction of the horse barn, but after about a quarter-mile, he turned left up the hill on to East River Road, which ran roughly parallel with 89. East River was much less traveled and offered a fairly safe course for the seasoned runner who could tax him or herself thoroughly on the rolling terrain before the road curved back to 89 about twenty-six miles north.

Once he got the kinks out, Fallon settled into the mental meanderings that typically characterized his morning workouts. He recalled Jessie's query, "What are ya hopin' to find?" *Good question,* he thought. Was he, as she had implied, really just smitten like a teenager over a silver-screen beauty who was about as accessible as Alpha Centauri? Kristin Scott Thomas was obviously integral to his fascination with *The Horse Whisperer,* regardless of the compelling storyline or the intriguing characters of Tom Booker and Annie Maclean. Or was it just the lure of Montana? As Fallon ran, he also thought about Jessie herself. How could someone with so much to offer still be single? No doubt, she had every Livingston cowboy in hot pursuit, but in spite of her western bent, maybe she was a little too urbane and bright under that rustic bearing to settle for one of the locals. At 32, she was hardly a spinster, but in light of her natural beauty and obvious erudition, Fallon thought she might just intimidate most of the provincial heroes. She was one-and-the-same the temptress and the carnivore. She could easily devour the unwary guy.

Fallon ran about four or five miles north on East River before turning around at a ranch entrance and retracing his route to his Dome Mountain cabin. By the time he returned, the activity around the lodge had subsided, and the group in the vans and all the fly fishermen were well on their way to their day's activities. He wondered again who the van riders were, but his curiosity left him as he trudged through the cabin door and crashed on his cot.

After a shower and a bowl of Cheerios, Fallon took Brandie for a walk in the foothills of the Gallatins, and then they both jumped in the Blazer and traveled north on the scenic East River Road. About eight miles north of where East River meets 89 by the Dome Mountain Lodge, Fallon rolled through Pray and discovered the Chico Hot Springs Resort and Day Spa. Chico Hot Springs was a verdant oasis in the midst of the rugged Absarokas. Converted from a miners' hospital in 1900, the resort was largely composed of impeccable white buildings, and it offered horseback riding, river rafting, fishing, massage therapy, dining, swimming, hiking, shopping, dog sledding, and drinking. He left Brandie in the Blazer and grabbed an Amstel Light and a small pizza at the very chic Chico Hot Springs Saloon. Although the bartender/server was most effusive, she remained fixed in her claims that she had no idea where any of the scenes from *The Horse Whisperer* were filmed. Fallon drank just enough beer to wash down his pizza, and then he headed for his cabin.

That evening, after a late afternoon nap, Fallon tried the Stockman's Restaurant in Livingston for dinner. The place was pretty much packed, even on a Tuesday night around 7:30. Since he was alone, however, Fallon was seated rather quickly. He ordered the baked chicken with wild rice, and even though the entrée was prominently located on the menu, the waitress looked at him like he had just committed the unpardonable sin in cattle country. The patrons seemed to be mostly married couples who knew each other. Fallon longed for the kind of life they led, rugged but even-paced and purposeful. He concluded intuitively that neither the patrons nor the employees would brook his inquiries into *The Horse Whisperer.*

On Wednesday, he and Brandie spent the day exploring the surroundings of the Dome Mountain Ranch and looking for any of the gravel roads that Annie Maclean had taken to the Booker Ranch. Although he was sure that a stretch of the Absarokas near Dome Mountain had been the backdrop for the horseback ride taken by Booker and Maclean, he could find no other visual evidence of the movie scenes. As he drove, he recalled the close-up Robert Redford had likely ordered of Kristin Scott Thomas seated on a rock. The simple beauty of her face and short, reddish hair was, to Fallon, stunning. Her facial expressions often said more than the script: anger, impatience, vulnerability, strength, and anguish. Without knowing that a Sean Fallon drew breath anywhere on the planet, she had completely mastered his psyche.

When he reached the northern end of East River, where it merged with 89, he took the U.S. route into Livingston to have lunch at another place Jessie had written on the note pad. The Pickle Barrel Sandwich Shop was as quaint as its name suggested, and it was patronized by a potpourri of people whose personas seemed to range from the pinstriped business brokers in power suits and pumps to the burly bronco busters in blue jeans and boots. All seemed to mingle easily and gregariously as they talked among themselves and wolfed down their meals. Over a Coke, a grilled cheese, and fries at the counter, Fallon asked what looked like the most authentic of cowboys on the stool next to him, "Do you know if the movie *The Horse Whisperer* was filmed around here?"

"Think so."

"Do you know exactly where?"

"Nope. Roscoe, where was *The Horse Whisperer* filmed?"

An equally genuine cowboy at a cloth-covered table responded without so much as a glance from his bean soup, "Damned if I know."

"Sorry," said the stool jockey.

"Thanks anyway."

On his way back to the ranch, the sky turned quickly black, and within minutes Fallon had to use his windshield wipers. By the time he reached the sign for Emigrant, sheets of water were engulfing his windshield so fast his wipers couldn't keep pace with the downpour. After he pulled into the driveway of the main lodge and parked near his cabin, he waited about five minutes with Brandie until the rain subsided a bit. He hustled Brandie into the cabin, and then made a break for the lobby of the lodge.

Renee was at the counter with her back to the door demonstrating a string trick for T. J., who was trying to figure out how she could release the string that encircled their hands without breaking the touch of their fingers. Over her shoulder she said to Fallon as he walked in, "Got caught in a gully washer, did ya?"

"Man, did it come in fast!"

T. J. waved hello to Fallon as he headed into the kitchen area after giving up on the string trick. Fallon had not taken

125

John Hagan

notice of what T. J. and Renee had been doing.

"Sean, I'll betcha five bucks the rain's completely outta here in ten minutes."

"Renee, did you see a turnip truck sputter down 89?"

"Nope. Didya fall offa one?"

"Maybe. But I'm still savvy enough not to bet on the local weather with a hustler like you."

"Hell, I thought I could at least nick you for the price of a good beer."

"Hey, I'm just a down-on-his-luck old re..."

"I know. I know. You want a job this winter?"

"Are you serious?"

"You'd get lodging and fifteen bucks an hour for utility work."

"Don't tempt me."

"Speakin' of temptation. Didya enjoy your ride with Jessie?"

"That's why I'm here. I'd like to try again tomorrow."

"Nine-thirty okay?"

"Great. I'll get a run in first."

"Keep your butt in the saddle, cowboy."

"Thanks, Renee!"

Fallon felt like he'd known Renee and T. J. all his life. With some people, you can just blend into their lives. The Deckers were perfect for the Dome Mountain Ranch.

Thursday morning was a little foggy and cooler than Wednesday, so Fallon wore a short-sleeved T-shirt over his long-sleeved one. He finished a quick five miles and jumped in the shower. He arrived at the horse barn around 9:20, wearing a university sweatshirt over a fresh long-sleeved T-shirt. Two horses were saddled and tied to the iron rail, but no one else seemed to be around.

"Jessie."

From inside the stables stepped Randy the fishing guide, who was obviously dressed for a horseback ride.

"Mornin', Randy! Uh, what's up?"

A Long Farewell

"I'm your wrangler this morning. Jessie's on a four-hour ride with two couples, so she couldn't take you today. She said to say hello, though. And she asked if you'd had any luck. Don't know what she meant by that."

Randy could read the disappointment on Fallon's face as easily as a first-grade primer, but he discreetly alluded to a bogus reason for Fallon's crestfallen expression.

"Don't worry. I'm really quite capable. I won't serve us to the grizzlies for lunch."

"Oh, yeah. No problem."

Randy was, in fact, more than quite capable. He was a great guide; he just wasn't...Jessie.

In spite of the overcast conditions and the nip of fall, the ride was still exhilarating, just not stimulating, titillating, fascinating, and palpitating.

When Fallon reached the cabin around noon, he took Brandie for a walk, but he tried to keep her from rock formations where rattlers might lurk. Returning to the cabin, he inhaled a peanut butter sandwich and a banana and washed them down with a bottle of Ruby Red grapefruit juice. He flopped on the cot and resumed work on one of the poems he was writing in his notebook, but he was fast asleep in twenty minutes. When he awakened around 7:00 p.m., he couldn't believe he'd practically slept the day away. It was nearly pitch dark, so he threw on some jeans, a sweatshirt, and his Justins and headed to the last place on Jessie's list, The Whiskey Creek Saloon. The place was teeming with life. C&W brayed out from the massive speakers, and the tables and chairs and bar stools were nearly all occupied. He was more than a little intimidated. He was sure everyone was staring at him and thinking he was Methuselah's older brother. By sheer chance or beginner's luck, he found an open stool at the bar, and when the very hot barmaid said, "Whatcha need, hon?" he nearly stammered, "Uh, ya have any Amstel Light on tap?"

"Comin' up."

When she brought him his beer, he handed her a ten, and she just said, "Thanks, cowboy!" and then resumed talking to some friends farther down the bar after she went to the cash register.

"Oh well."

Fallon figured there must have been at least fifty people in the bar who could tell him just about anything regarding *The Horse Whisperer*, but (A) he didn't have the chutzpah to bring it up in The Whiskey Creek because (B) he'd only get the now-familiar glazed stare or maybe that thunderstruck look of selective amnesia.

He ordered another ten-dollar beer and had nearly finished it in a perfect state of melancholy when a beautiful hand reached around him and lifted his remaining suds. By the time he turned on the stool, he found Jessie draining the last two or three gulps from his glass.

"Ya look pretty good on that stool for an old English teacher. Didya catch up with Kristin yet?"

Fallon took a deep breath. Jessie was in a pair of designer jeans and a skin-tight, blue top that didn't quite reach her beltline. Her high-heeled boots made her look like she was about six-feet tall.

"Damn, it's good to see you!"

He had completely blown his reserve.

"You too, Sean Fallon! Sorry I couldn't take you today."

Not nearly as sorry as I was, thought Fallon.

"Just my bad luck."

"Well, we're about to change it, cowboy." She hollered at the barmaid, "Hey, Brenda."

"Whatcha need, Jess?"

"Where exactly did they shoot most of *The Horse Whisperer?*"

"Around the 63, out offa Swingley."

"Thanks, babe! Owe ya one."

Jessie flashed her big pearlies at Brenda but turned to Fallon and frowned.

"Listen, I'm with some people right now or I'd sit here with ya all night. And I've got another two-hour in the morning, but..."

"Oh, that's okay. I'll just..."

"Listen to me. We're goin' out at eight, so I'll pick you up at your cabin around eleven, and we'll find some scenes from that damned movie for you and maybe some reminders of Kristin. But you're buyin' lunch!"

"You're on! You're not too bad for an Equestrian Studies major."

She just turned and walked away, patting her gorgeous butt and suggesting he could just kiss it.

Around 11:20 on Friday morning, Jessie pulled up in a dusty, red Jeep Wrangler and banged on Fallon's cabin door. The sun had returned in full force and was radiant in the clear blue sky, but the temperature was still only in the low 60's, so she was dressed in her Lee jeans, Ariat boots, raffia hat, and faded sweatshirt over a personalized T-shirt. She had come straight from the horse barn, and she was hungry.

Before Fallon could open the door, she yelled, "C'mon Sean, I'm starvin'."

Fallon and Brandie came to the door and found the embodiment of vitality and motion standing before them. Fallon wasn't sure who had more energy, Brandie the Border Collie or Jessie the whirling dervish.

"Let's go. You drivin'?"

"Yep. But you're buyin'. I thought those people'd never stop talkin'."

Fallon just laughed and jumped in the passenger seat, and Brandie hopped into the back. They stopped at the convenience store in Emigrant and bought some ham sandwiches and potato chips and sloshed them down with Dr. Peppers.

"Where we headed?"

"Out to the 63 Ranch on Bruffey Lane."

"You're the boss."

As they drove, Jessie maintained a non-stop travelogue, signaling points of interest along the way. Swingley Road was a partially asphalt, partially gravel byway that offered several possibilities of where Annie Maclean pulled her Range Rover to a stop and read from her directions to the Booker Ranch while she marveled at the sheer beauty of the mountains and open range. Fallon was snapping pictures along the way, asking Jessie to stop repeatedly. She accommodated him patiently, which surprised him somewhat. Just when he thought he had captured a view from the movie, they'd drive over another rise, and he'd be sure that "this is the one."

It wasn't until they turned on to Bruffey Lane that they came up over a slight grade and he almost yelled, "Stop, here!"

Looking through the windshield, he was fairly certain that he was now in nearly the exact spot where Kristin Scott Thomas, as Annie Maclean, had gazed with wonder upon the gravel road that stretched before her and led to a seemingly endless expanse of fence line and pasture land, bedecked with bluish, snow-capped mountains. He recalled Redford's skillfully captured scene in which the bespectacled Annie, holding the note card with her directions, stared out the window in confusion and amazement. Her crimson lips were slightly parted, as again her facial expression augmented the beholder's understanding of the power and grandeur of a quintessentially Montana view. As Fallon absorbed this profound moment, he knew that Redford had rendered the spectacle perfectly.

Jessie allowed him to shoot several pictures before interjecting her own emotions and impressions.

"I just love autumn in Montana, but the season goes so quickly."

"I love autumn just about anywhere, but I believe the movie scenes were shot in the spring to remain consistent with the novel."

130

"Well, they should have shot the movie in the fall, anyway."

"You're right. They should've."

He smiled at her, and she responded with a smile that made his seem feeble. She leaned over and kissed him, and he responded with a look of total astonishment and delight.

"Too bad you belong to Kristin. Being here with you at this spot at my favorite time of the year is very special. You're an intriguing guy, Sean Fallon. Strange, but intriguing."

He had no response: nothing witty, nothing literary, and nothing clever.

They drove past the 63 Ranch and shot some pictures, and then they found some more sites that looked like scenes from the movie. Throughout the day they exchanged some lively repartee, and Fallon discovered even more of the lightning wit of this dazzling young woman. When they pulled up to his cabin around seven o'clock, Jessie put the Wrangler in neutral and said, "Thanks, Sean, for allowing me to be a part of your *Horse Whisperer* day. It was one of the best times I've ever had. An autumn day has taken on a new meaning for me."

Casting caution and convention aside, he leaned over and kissed her.

"I need to get out of here before I do or say something really stupid. C'mon, Brandie."

He shut the passenger-side door of the Wrangler and put his left palm on the window. He turned and walked into the cabin. He had told Jessie he was leaving Dome Mountain around 9:00 in the morning. That night, he worked especially hard in his notebook.

By 8:00 on Saturday morning, Fallon had showered and packed. He walked over to the main lodge to pay the bill for lodging and horseback riding. When he walked into the lobby, Renee was twirling the circular string she had used for the trick with T. J.

"Morning, Renee. I guess it's time for me to pay the piper."

"I really do hate to see you go, Sean. You've been kind of a novelty around here."

"You really mean whacko."

"Well, I'm too much of a lady to call you that."

Smirking, she turned to slide his credit card through the machine. As he was signing the billing receipt, Renee asked him, "Hey, you ever tried this string trick?"

"What string trick?"

"Well, we hold our fingers together with this string around..."

"Where'd you learn that trick?"

Renee knew she was in deep water.

"That's the string trick used in *The Horse Whisperer*."

Renee came clean.

"Actually, Sean, the string is kind of a souvenir-gift."

"From whom?"

"Well, I guess it doesn't matter now. Didn't you notice that group of people leaving and arriving at the lodge for the past week?"

"Yeah, I did. I meant to ask..."

"I'm surprised you didn't see her."

"Who?"

"Kristin Scott Thomas. She was here all week with a company shooting a documentary on the Absaroka Indians. I'm sorry, Sean, but we were asked not to discuss their identity. They left this morning around seven for the Bozeman airport."

"And the string, she..."

"It was one of several she said they used as props for *The Horse Whisperer*. When I asked her how the movie trick worked, she demonstrated the technique and gave me the string."

"Unbelievable!"

"You know what? I'll bet she'd want you to have it."

Renee handed the string to Fallon.

"Aw, no, Renee. I couldn't..."

"Take it, cowboy. It'll make my day."

"You're the best, Renee!"

"Thanks, sweetie! Come back and see us again."

Fallon started toward the door but stopped abruptly.

"Would you mind givin' this to Jessie?"

He handed her a small envelope.

"Be glad to."

"Bye."

Around 8:30 a.m., Jessie burst through the door of the lodge lobby and yelled to Renee, who was back in the kitchen.

"Where's Fallon?"

Stepping to the counter, Renee said, "He's gone, hon."

Jessie just stood there with her mouth slightly agape, and then muttered, "But he said he wasn't leaving until nine."

"I couldn't tell you about that, but he left you this."

Renee handed her the envelope.

"Thanks."

After Fallon merged on to I-90 from U.S. 89, he began twisting the looped black string that looked like just a shoelace. Thinking fondly that Annie Maclean had done the same as she drove from the Booker Ranch, he fantasized that Kristin Scott Thomas had given it to him.

Sitting in her Wrangler in the parking lot of the Dome Mountain Lodge, Jessica Lynn Kearney read the contents of the envelope:

John Hagan

Autumn Day

You dazzle me with colors as I walk.
Each hour the sunlight changes your bright hues.
The breeze exhilarates me as I stalk
The quarry of your rich, fantastic views.
Conditions are so perfect while you stay.
Your splendor seems quite boundless and surreal.
With my keen senses you will have your way;
My thoughts of all that matters you will steal.
Your blue skies and white clouds go hand-in-hand.
Jack Frost has worked his magic on each leaf.
Your radiance explodes upon the land,
But pulchritude is wayward and so brief.
Before old Father Time does turn the page,
You'll "strut and [primp your] hour upon the stage."*

Beneath his sonnet, Fallon wrote: "Jessie, It's been a long while since I've been anyone's 'best time.' Your cowboy buddy, Sean."

For the first time in over a year or two, Jessie wept.

*Macbeth—William Shakespeare

134

A Long Farewell

Howsoever these things be,
A long farewell to Locksley Hall!
Now for me the woods may wither,
Now for me the roof-tree fall.

—***Locksley Hall***
Alfred, Lord Tennyson

At about 3:45 p.m. on a beautiful late-September day, Brendan Farrell turned in his desk chair in the principal's office to look out upon the manicured front lawn of the award-winning Maplemont High School. As he did, he observed the approach of his boss, an egocentric man whose every action supported his need to apprise his subordinates that he was, indeed, their superintendent.

Dr. James L. Kline had arrived at the Maplemont City Schools three years before, bearing a reputation as a hatchet man on a mission and an ego inversely proportionate to his smallish wingtips. Uncommonly smart and fearlessly brash, Kline had taken an immediate dislike to Brendan because of the principal's aversion to his leadership style. The past three years had begun with Kline's veiled threats to fire Brendan but had evolved into an uneasy peace, owing to Brendan's compliance with the superintendent's authority and Kline's hope that if he were patient, Brendan would retire and be out of his flowing flaxen locks. Brendan regarded Kline as bit of a charlatan who purloined his administrators' ideas and then offered them as his own when he addressed the board or the community. Brendan could be an opportunistic cad himself, but in the self-centered Kline he found little of the endearing.

Brendan knew from experience that Kline was headed for

his office, so he immediately stepped around the corner and notified his secretary, Jackie Norris, that she might as well leave since it was nearly four o'clock and her superintendent was on his way into the building. Jackie simply rolled her eyes, knowing that the sooner she left, the fewer condescending remarks she would have to endure from the most imperious man she had ever known professionally. Brendan loved to taunt Jackie with references to "your superintendent" because they allowed him to disenfranchise himself from Kline and affix his boss directly upon Norris as a kind of occupational albatross. Kline was always complimentary to Jackie; it was his tone and irrepressible need to preface nearly every comment to her with "as your superintendent, Jackie" that really fueled her ire.

Jackie was a foxy forty-three-year-old divorcee, but she rarely, if ever, seemed to be using her comeliness to gain an edge. Brendan had hired her two years before because her interview revealed a woman of glib speech, direct responses, and eminent qualifications. The fact that she was pretty much drop-dead gorgeous hadn't damaged her chances, but Brendan came to discover that what he suspected of her capabilities during her interview didn't hint at the quick-studied efficiency she actually brought to the position.

Brendan watched through the glass of the double doors as Jackie walked out and greeted Kline in the hallway. He almost knew the very text of her exchange. As smooth as silk, she'd blow smoke up Kline's butt and make him even more pompous than he was already.

Seconds later, Kline entered Brendan's office and broached his conversation with the usual vapid amenities.

"It's just a gorgeous fall day, isn't it."

"Yeah, and tomorrow's forecast calls for a beautiful night for the game."

"Middleton'll bring a huge crowd. I want the grounds in exquisite condition."

"Jim, the grounds always look great. The service guys do

an excellent job."

"They do since I made them. You know, I shouldn't have to be the one to do that. I know you like those guys, but that's another place where you let your friendships get in the way of your responsibilities."

"Right."

"By the way, have you begun to document Sperry's deficiencies yet? I want that A. P. Chemistry program in place by next year, and I don't want him teaching it."

"We met yesterday to set his goals for the year."

"I want you to set his goals for him, and I don't want any wiggle room for him to forestall his removal from those chem classes. If he won't leave, we'll move him to the junior high or assign him to a full schedule of physical science."

"Jim, I'm not thrilled with John's work either, but dammit, I didn't hire him, and I didn't recommend him for tenure. For too many years around here, tenure was as automatic as a first grader movin' to second. I'll write an evaluation based on his performance, but if the union's convinced that he's bein' screwed, the shit'll hit the fan."

"Brendan, I've already talked with Martin, and he knows the community has had it with Sperry. There'll be no problem with the union, only the nominal inquiries about procedural requirements."

"All right."

"I've got to go. I'm addressing a Rotary Club dinner group tonight. See you tomorrow."

"Enjoy your dinner."

Kline stopped in the doorway. "You know how these things are. I've got to kiss the babies and stroke the movers and shakers so the rest of you can just do your jobs."

"Yeah, right."

Kline dashed out the door of the outer office, and Brendan watched him approach the gregarious Denver Walsh, one of the night service crew.

Walsh was a tree-trunk of a man who stood about 5'6"

tall and weighed about 240 pounds. He had legs that looked like fire hydrants and forearms that looked like Popeye's. With a lower lip packed with Skoal and dressed in a ball cap, T-shirt, knee-length shorts, and high-topped work shoes, he was mankind's equivalent of R2-D2. A quintessentially good-natured country boy, he would often listen to Kline patiently and later laugh boisterously with Brendan or others while telling a makeshift joke with Kline as either the cuckolded lover or clueless dupe in his fabliau. Some of Brendan's best times in education were spent with the fun-loving people like Walsh.

Geez, Brendan thought, *Kline just goes from pillar-to-post micro managing and asserting authority.*

In spite of his personal disagreements with Kline, Brendan did acknowledge publicly, and for that matter privately, his boss had effected needed and meaningful changes in the district. He had through various means greatly enhanced the historical buildings and beautiful grounds throughout the system, and he had forced the faculties from the comforts of an ever-increasing complacency. He was, of course, right about Brendan; he wasn't tough enough on weak employees, and he had gotten too close to some. Brendan knew that someone needed to force some issues, and Kline, for all of Brendan's aversion to him, was willing to be the curmudgeon when circumstances required. Much of what Brendan disliked about Kline was actually grounded in a peculiar respect for the superintendent's uncompromising abrasiveness and swagger.

With Kline gone, Brendan grabbed his gym bag out of the closet, pulled down the shades of his office, and jumped into a T-shirt, sweat pants, and gym shoes for his three-day-a-week weight room workout. It was truly a magnificent day, and he'd do an abbreviated routine to enjoy as much of the declining fall daylight as possible.

As he made his way along the corridor, he marveled again, as he had so often, at the artistic skills of the students who had provided a masterful rendering of Franz Kafka's character, Gregor Samsa, from *The Metamorphosis* on the wall at the end of the hallway. Spanning the visible wall space at the end of the hall, Gregor cast his knowing gaze upon all who traveled in the passageway he commanded. The black eyes of Gregor the insect created the disturbing impression that they followed you as you walked down the hallway and turned the corner. Gregor's stare reminded Brendan of F. Scott Fitzgerald's description of Doctor T. J. Eckleburg's eyes in *The Great Gatsby*. Like the billboard eyes of Eckleburg, Gregor's eyes seemed to see into the very mind of the passerby. Brendan suspected that Gregor knew what you were thinking; he knew your self-serving motives, your petty jealousies, your cowardly fears, your private hostilities, and your shameless lusts. Brendan sometimes followed a curvaceous female teacher down the hall under the scrutiny of Gregor, who knew that the cute toosh that swayed back and forth was the principal's wanton fancy.

When Brendan entered the weight room, he was greeted by Gary Bensman, who was already well into his workout and had a nice sweat going.

"I'm way ahead of ya, little man. Where the hell've ya been?"

At even a slouching 6'4", Gary towered over Brendan's 5'10", but he knew that the wiry principal could hold his own with just about anyone on the staff in the high school weight room.

Bensman was the long-time English Department chairman, and he had become an institution in and of himself, owning as he did a reputation as a wonderfully well-versed and skillful classroom presenter. He taught the senior advanced placement classes and was frequently key to the success of essays required in student applications to the Ivies, Northwestern, Notre Dame, Stanford, Vanderbilt, and others deemed "most competitive" by college and university guidebooks. Based on his physical stature, classroom reputation, and rakishly good looks, Bensman was one of the most prepossessing people Brendan had ever met in the ranks of high school teaching. He neither asked any quarter from nor gave any quarter to those whom he held in contempt, and he seemingly feared no authority. Brendan likened him to the harpooner Queequeg in Herman Melville's *Moby Dick* because Bensman was to Maplemont High School what Queequeg was to the *Pequod*. He had no real authority, but he took no guff from anyone.

"I got held up by Kline," answered Brendan, tossing his weight belt on to a chair.

"You need to tell that pain in the ass you've got more important things to attend. Why doesn't the board give him something to do so he'll stay out of the buildings?"

"Who knows?"

As Brendan began some light work on the bench, he was in and out of thoughts about his latest meeting with Kline and what he would do about John Sperry. John was a knowledgeable young science teacher, but he had struggled with classroom dynamics at the beginning of his Maplemont experience, and he was working in a community that was long on memory and short on tolerance. Owing to his subject of choice and his given name, Maplemont students didn't take long to christen him "Chem John."

Brendan remembered all too well a similar experience in his first year as a principal at Browning, a small high school in a rather depressed district in Northwestern Ohio. Grace Miller, the young instrumental music teacher, had preceded him to Browning by three years, and she was struggling to save her job under deplorable conditions. From the superintendent, who was under pressure from the board president, Brendan had been given his marching orders to begin the process of the teacher's non-renewal almost from the moment he arrived.

Grace was married to a rarely employed trumpet player, and she carried most of the financial burden for herself, her husband, and her two-year-old daughter. Her band room, which was located directly above Brendan's office, was a converted study hall and an acoustical nightmare. Brendan was the victim of the clangs and thuds of cymbals and drums every day after lunch during fifth period. The raucous sounds from above, mixed with the gastric distress from generic peanut butter, grapefruit juice, and macaroni, produced at least one migraine per week. Grace's allotment of instruments, equipment, and sheet music was disgraceful, and the medium for her marching band's performances was a postage-stamp-sized gymnasium. Browning had no football team and thus no field on which nor event during which the band could march in formations; therefore, so-called marching band performances took place on cold winter nights during the halftimes of basketball games. Band parents hung around for the show, but most folks hit the hallways for a pee or a popcorn. Hers was a *fait accompli*, of course, and no matter what efforts Grace made, certain forces in the community had decided her fate. One of those forces was the board president whose daughter had received a second-chair rating on clarinet for her senior year in the concert band in spite of her mother's machinations to effect a first-chair rating.

Brendan remembered the poignant scene in his office that spring when he had told Grace that she would not be retained as the band director. As she pleaded her case, Brendan realized how profoundly victimized she had been by circumstances, which included him. He tried to console himself with the rationalization that he was only doing what he was directed to do and that Grace's fate was sealed before he arrived. Anyway, what was he to do as a rookie principal trying to establish himself in the ranks of administration? The truth was that he had been a craven pawn who should have said "No, in thunder" and cleaned out his desk. When Grace said, "I thought you were different. I thought I could count on you," she stripped away every vestige of his administrative bearing, and from that point forward, his part of the dialogue was little more than evasive drivel.

Strangely, all teacher evaluations he had conducted since were in some way influenced by his experience with Grace Miller. Lurking behind every critique was the suspicion that he was reacting to student or parent complaints, personality clashes, professional envy, district politics, community disposition, or, worst of all, ugly prejudice. Who in the hell was he as one of the most flawed people on the planet to sit in judgment of those trying to make a living?

***

At about 4:10 p.m. on December 9, Brendan was seated before his computer working on his mid-year evaluation of John Sperry and his recommendations for the chemistry teacher's future performance. He had conducted two formal observations of Sperry to date, in addition to a number of casual walk-by's and drop-in's. Brendan's problem in evaluating Sperry was in qualifying and quantifying the abstract, immeasurable elements of teaching. Student responsiveness, interest, and enthusiasm were difficult to establish other than obliquely through enrollment numbers that could be influenced by many factors. Knowing that the heat was on from parents and thus from the superintendent, Sperry was careful to dot his I's and cross his T's in class presentations, adherence to course of study, response to pupil and parent concerns, and completion of reports and referrals.

Although Brendan rarely had contact with the thirty-six-year-old Sperry beyond the school setting, he liked John personally and knew that he was a conscientious teacher and a genuinely humane person. Like anyone else he had some idiosyncrasies that were a bit discomforting, but he was always respectful and friendly in an offbeat sort of way. His left eye wandered, and in conversation it could be somewhat distracting, since John was one of those people who quite unconsciously stood uncomfortably close to others. Indeed, some students and parents had complained of this habit, implying that the behavior was on the periphery of physical intimidation. Brendan knew better, but it was just another rationale for student and parent criticism of Sperry's teaching. Parent phone calls would often allude plaintively to the tenure laws in Ohio, which in their view practically guaranteed teachers lifetime employment. While the tenets of tenure did force administrators to be more aggressive and analytical in evaluating weak teachers, Brendan, in spite of his own understanding of continuing contracts, defended them in conversations with parents, reasoning that they only provided due process for teachers and prevented arbitrary and capricious non-renewals.

John Sperry regularly made himself available as a chaperone for dances and other school events, and Brendan called upon him frequently to pick up extra duties throughout the school day because John would do so without consulting the master contract to determine if he was required. He had also accepted the advisorship of the National Honor Society chapter, a low paying supplemental position that offered many headaches and little thanks. All of these factors contributed to Brendan's frustration because John hadn't won student endorsement or made chemistry viable. He was a master of his subject but an apprentice in the classroom. Brendan had run out of suggestions, and Kline was watching closely.

Shortly after the next morning's announcements, Jackie sent the call in to Brendan from Jim Kline, who notified his principal that he was on his way from the central office to talk about John Sperry. He arrived about ten minutes later, and, eschewing his customary exchanges with Jackie, he marched directly into Brendan's office and came immediately to the point.

"Brendan, I need to know exactly where you are with Sperry."

"I finished the rough draft of his mid-year late yesterday. Wanna read it?"

"No. Just give me the basics."

Something in Kline's tone suggested that the superintendent was beginning to understand Brendan's dilemma regarding John Sperry. In fact, Brendan thought he detected some improvement in his relationship with Kline.

"Well then, basically I'm telling him that he's made every effort to provide first-rate instruction for all of his students, but..."

"But?"

"But he continues to lose ground in terms of student interest in and enthusiasm for chemistry."

"When do you plan to sit down with him?"

"Sometime after Christmas but before exams."

"I'd agree with that, but how do you think he'll take it?"

"I'd guess he'll argue that he can turn things around by the end of the year."

"Brendan, the board's prepared to approve the A. P. Chemistry for next year at the February meeting, but three of them have already expressed their reservations about John's teaching it. You need to be quite clear with him as to where you're headed with chemistry next year."

"I was planning to tell him in January that I may have to reassign him next year."

"No. Tell him that in all likelihood you will be reassigning him next year. And put that in writing."

"I wouldn't expect it from John, but he could just go in the tank for the rest of the year if he thinks there's no hope for chemistry."

"Then do your job, Brendan, and document carefully. If that happens, we'll deal with it in April."

For some reason Brendan didn't take Kline's remark as an affront. He knew that Kline was in the hot seat too and that someone had to make difficult decisions. Kline seemed to have mellowed some through the fall, and Brendan suspected that his superintendent was trying to get outside himself and extend the olive branch. They'd never be buddies, but Brendan was beginning to see more of the man than was immediately evident. In fact, Kline was becoming almost likeable in his egotistical way.

"All right."

"You seem unsure."

"It's just that I've always questioned my right to affect people's lives that way."

"Brendan, it's not your right; it's your responsibility. In a position of your influence, you've got to take yourself more seriously."

Brendan considered Kline's possible reaction to his next remark, thinking that the superintendent might take it as a not-so-veiled recommendation for his own deportment, which, of course, it was.

" 'Angels fly because they take themselves so lightly.' "

"How's that?"

"G. K. Chesterton."

"Touché! See you later."

Brendan decided that he needed to get out of the office for a while, so he told Jackie he'd be wandering the halls for the next half hour or so, a luxury of the principalship that he enjoyed a great deal and that he knew his teachers probably envied. He often thought that like T. S. Eliot's J. Alfred Prufrock, whose life was measured out in coffee spoons, classroom teachers' lives were measured out in school bells. But for all of its headaches, the principalship did allow for significant latitude in terms of time use during the school day. Naturally, some things had to be done on schedule or by a certain hour, but to a large extent, the completion of a principal's quotidian duties was at his or her discretion or choice.

He walked up to the third floor, past the math and social studies classes, and tuned in on discussions ranging from the variables of Constitutional guarantees to the absolutes of

algebraic laws. He often marveled at the aggregate store of
genius and information that was available in any high school
in which specialized individuals brought their expertise to
bear in disciplines ranging from music to math, science to
social studies, fine arts to foreign language, library science to
language arts, wood working to wise shopping, and body
hygiene to business letters.

He knew he'd miss all of it someday, even the smells of
the classrooms: the chalk dust, the desk oil, and the cleaning
fluids. His teachers were a variegation of talents and person-
alities, each with his or her skill levels and capabilities.
Everyday, they left their respective homes and assembled at
Maplemont to make some brick and mortar a place of discovery and challenge to over 700 kids, for whom, good or bad,
high school could well be the defining experience in their
lives. Everyday, no matter what problems or distress they
might endure personally, his staff members put a face on
their own worries and functioned *in loco parentis* for kids
who brought their own sets of conflicts and anxieties into
this microcosm of the community. As cynical as he was himself at times and as weary as he could be at the end of a day,
Brendan knew that this was his medium. He never aspired
to anything else in a serious way, and he couldn't imagine
himself in any other profession or pursuit; he had no apti-
tude for any other work.

He ambled into the teachers' lounge, or "workroom" as
some euphemistically called it, where four or five of his staff
members were at various stages of industry, ranging from
sound asleep on an old couch to running tests on the copy
machine. He was immediately accosted by the portly Dustin
Foxworth, whose girth and condition disguised the fact that
on a golf course and with a six-pack already in him he could,
with extraordinary consistency, run a Maxfli or a Titleist up
within ten feet of the cup from ninety yards out. His acerbic
wit surpassed anything Brendan had ever known, and this
self-styled Jack Falstaff's litany of jokes stretched "out to the

crack of doom.'" He was truly a gifted though sarcastic English teacher who taxed his students to their absolute limits. While anyone was fair game for his invective, no quarry pleased him more than a passing administrator. Brendan would have enjoyed the barbs more if he had been able to match Foxworth in literary repartee.

"Well, I see that our sinecure-blessed principal has deigned to join the proletarian masses in their squalid environs."

Brendan wanted to make some rejoinder related to the antiquity of Foxworth's last carnal contact with a woman, but with the prudish Madeleine Stelzer and Helen Kahn present, he was rather restricted in his caustic options.

"Actually, I just dropped in to observe how much 'work' was taking place in the teachers' workroom."

Brendan deposited some coins into the fruit drink machine and retrieved a small bottle of his daily orange juice fix.

"You can't observe a teacher's 'spontaneous overflow of powerful feelings, recollected in tranquility.' "

"Maybe, but I doubt that Wordsworth had your lazy butt in mind when he was defending poetry."

"No, but Hamlet probably had an administrator in mind when he referred to a 'wretched, rash intruding fool.' "

Brendan knew he was licked again, so he mouthed "up yours," which he knew Foxworth could lip-read but the others couldn't see. As he walked toward the door, Brendan could hear Foxworth say, "Ladies, our principal is a loathsome Philistine." Brendan couldn't see them, of course, but he knew that Stelzer and Kahn wouldn't know whether to protest, agree, or go straight up and scatter.

Brendan no sooner hit the hallway than a voice hailed him from behind.

"Hey, I've been lookin' for you. Where ya been?"

It was his assistant principal, Frank Blankenship.

"Hidin' from walkin' problems like you."

147

"Well, I've got one. It's Darrell Rhodes again, and he's in my office. You have time to talk to him with me?"

"Nope. I'm on break right now."

"What's the matter? Ya just go another round or two with Foxworth? He put another wuppin' on ya, didn't he."

"Let's go."

Although Frank Blankenship was Brendan's assistant principal, he wore every hat imaginable. He was also the athletics director and attendance officer. In a school Maplemont's size, an assistant principal and athletics director as separate entities would have been protested by the taxpayers and the teachers' union, so in addition to his other responsibilities, Frank helped Brendan with disciplinary matters, especially at the preliminary stages.

Brendan and Frank entered the assistant principal's outer office and walked past Laura Hastings and Vicki Vagedes, the two secretaries who handled the phone calls, visitors, and paper work for athletics, attendance, and anything else related to Frank's myriad duties. Vicki just leaned her head in the direction of Frank's office, where Darrell Rhodes slouched in a visitor's chair in front of the assistant principal's desk.

Rhodes was atypical of the cookie-cutter Maplemont students who often spent piles of their parents' money to look slovenly in designer clothes. He was routinely dressed in army fatigues and combat boots. The dress code prevented his wearing an insignia or a hat in the building, but his garb was unmistakably martial and set him conspicuously apart from mainstream Maplemont. As an eighteen-year-old junior, he was older than most of the seniors and had few if any real friends. At 6'2" and about 175 pounds, he was rangy at best, but his physical maturity made him an imposing figure to most of the underclassmen, an advantage he exploited at every opportunity. He was wily enough to avoid confrontations with his physical equals, but he maintained his image as a hard case at all times.

A Long Farewell

Rhodes was from a family of two children. He had a sister in one of the elementaries who was as cooperative and pleasant as her brother was belligerent and bellicose. Although he paid rent from a part-time job at a bowling alley, Darrell lived with his sister Rhonda and their mother, who was estranged from her husband. Buying a bungalow on the outskirts of the district at what for her was a prohibitive purchase price, Mrs. Donna Rhodes had moved her children from the inner city to provide her kids with a more advantageous environment, a cultural and academic gain for Rhonda but a benefit entirely lost upon Darrell. Little was known about the kids' father, Bart Rhodes, other than he had purportedly been dishonorably discharged from the United States Army and showed up periodically to disrupt most of what Donna had been able to accomplish for the kids. Word from Darrell's previous high school was that Bart would invariably be present at any suspension hearing for Darrell to protest the inequities of the disciplinary code and decry his son's bum deal.

"Darrell, I've asked Mr. Farrell to sit in on this discussion because he's aware that I've already assigned you three Saturday Schools for the same kind of complaint Mitchell Shapiro has made against you today."

"Yeah, well where's Shapiro and what's he sayin'?"

"He says that as he was stepping away from his locker, you grabbed him from behind and threw him into another student and that the two of their heads collided, leaving a bump above Mitch's left eye."

Amused by the image, Rhodes laughed and said, "What makes 'im think I did it?"

"Three or four other students saw you. What were you doing in the freshman hall anyway? You don't have any business there."

"I was lookin' fer a fren."

"Which friend?"

"I ferget. Was a long time ago."

John Hagan

Frank and Brendan cast furtive glances at each other before the assistant principal proceeded.

"You forget, huh. Well, I haven't forgotten that this is the fourth freshman you've assaulted since you started here in August."

"I didn't assault nobody. Besides, Jason Williams is a southmore."

"In any case you've already had three Saturday Schools, which you know are in lieu of suspensions. I've tried to avoid suspensions for you because they'd result in zeros in all of your classes for the days you'd be out."

"Who's Lou?"

Rhodes laughed again, thinking he had gotten off an original. At this point Brendan broke in.

"Lou's a substitute for Joe Suspension, and as of now Lou's on a permanent vacation, leavin' you to deal with the first string. Mr. Blankenship's given you more chances than I would, Mr. Rhodes, and I'm putting you on notice that you're officially suspended for three days, beginning the day after tomorrow."

"The only Mr. Rhodes I know's my dad, and I know you can't suspend me without notifyin' him first."

"How old are you, Darrell?"

"Eighteen."

"Bingo!"

Rhodes guessed that as an emancipated eighteen-year-old in Ohio, his parents would not have to be notified, so he didn't press the point.

"You know, of course, you'll receive a written statement of my intent to suspend you, and as a courtesy I'll send the actual suspension notice to your mother. I'll have Mrs. Norris send for you later today so you can sign the intent to suspend."

"And what if I refuse to sign it?"

"I'll note that on the intent form and file it. Any questions?"

150

"Guess not."

When Brendan returned to his office, he told Jackie to type the specific information on to the two forms he needed to suspend Darrell Rhodes and then send for him whenever she had time. She was already inundated with work, and within the last hour had received three parent calls regarding "concerns" about teachers.

"I can't turn you loose for forty-five minutes without your getting into trouble."

"Just doin' my job, ma'am, just doin' my job."

Jackie could tell he was vexed, so she didn't jerk his chain too much. She had learned to read him so well that she knew when to spoof him out of a funk or when to salve his wounds with just the right counsel.

"I'll get on it right away."

"When you have time. I know you're buried."

Brendan made a couple of phone calls, and in the middle of the second, Jackie walked in and laid the two forms for him to sign on his desk and mouthed, "Darrell's here." Brendan just watched her walk out and wondered again how someone who looked and moved like a Lamborghini could work and perform like a John Deere.

***

By mid January the Maplemont High School staff and students had turned their attentions to exam week and the suspension of regular classes for the three days of tensions that students always felt no matter how often teachers encouraged them to relax.

Having already met with six other staff members on comprehensive evaluation to discuss their mid-year review of formal observations, Brendan had failed in his resolve to meet with John Sperry immediately after the holidays to discuss the chemistry teacher's progress.

At 10:30 a.m. on Thursday of exam week, Jackie called

in to Brendan to let him know that John Sperry had arrived for the meeting Brendan had delayed as long as possible.

"Brendan, John's here for his appointment. Should I send him in?"

"Only if you'd like to handle the meeting. How'd you like to use some of that Norris charm and do your dog-and-pony show back here for a while?"

"I don't think so."

Brendan knew that John was probably standing right next to Jackie's desk and that her jackass boss had just put her in another situation where she had to ad-lib a response to one of his asinine or ribald remarks about the person waiting to see him.

"Well, in that case I'll be out in a minute. You know what they say about rats, don't ya?"

"Uh, no."

"They leave a sinkin' ship first."

"I understand. I'll make a note of that."

Brendan used the next minute or so to review for the umpteenth time what he had written as a mid-year evaluation and recommendation for John Sperry. As difficult as writing evaluations and recommendations could be, sitting across the desk from the recipient while he or she read the document could be even more difficult. Even criticism couched in praise was often perceived by the teacher as a personal affront, and the glowing parts of the evaluation were often ignored by teachers who saw only the recommendations for improvement.

Brendan got up, opened the door, and greeted the anxious Sperry.

"Morning, John! How ya doin'?"

Better than you, Norris thought.

"Uh, fine," Sperry said.

Sperry took a chair across from Brendan, and the principal handed him the evaluation.

"John, why don't you look that over, and then we can

take our time to discuss it."

Sperry read the document carefully and slowly as Brendan tried to act as nonchalant as possible. The teacher's facial expressions said it all, even before he finished reading and responded verbally. His dismay was obvious, and Brendan knew that the moment of truth had arrived, regardless of his efforts to forestall it until spring.

"Brendan, you say here that you're planning to take my chemistry classes away from me. I don't believe that's fair."

"John, I'm saying that I'll likely reassign you to a physical and environmental science schedule. I'm not taking away your chemistry classes."

Brendan knew his response was a load of crap.

"C'mon, Brendan, you know that chemistry's my thing. I love teaching it; that's why I'm here."

"John, you were hired partly because of your comprehensive certification. Your versatility is one of your strengths. I don't see this as a compromise of your science knowledge. I simply need you in a different assignment. You know as well as I do that it wouldn't be a bad schedule, that it'll put you in a much less stressful situation."

"Less stressful for me or for you and Dr. Kline?"

"I won't argue that there's pressure out there on me and Jim, and you and I have talked about some of the board members' impatience. In fairness to Dr. Kline, I really believe he's run as much interference for you as he can. He's used all his trump cards."

"Why don't you stand in there for me?"

"John, I have. I take no pleasure in this."

For the next forty-five minutes Sperry and Farrell rehashed all the efforts John had made to improve his chemistry classes. John was a strong and logical self-advocate whose arguments made a great deal of sense, but no level of his reasoning obviated the simple fact that chemistry students at Maplemont were far from the delight in the spontaneous discovery that the truly dynamic science teacher could imbue in his or her students.

"Well, you say here that in all likelihood you'll be reassigning me to a physical and environmental science schedule next year."

"Yes."

"Then I'll redouble my efforts to improve my instruction between now and when you build the master schedule in when, March or April?"

"I'll start in March."

"I'll change your mind about this plan unless you're telling me to quit trying?"

"No. I'm not telling you that, John. But please know that the die may be cast."

"It ain't over 'til the fat lady sings, is it?"

"Uh, no."

Sperry signed his mid-year, and Brendan made him a copy. When the teacher walked out, Brendan knew that in the space of about an hour his whole relationship with John had been radically altered. John had regarded him as an advocate, but Brendan was now just another administrator covering his ass and using a teacher as fodder for his career.

Brendan got up from his desk and stood in front of the window. The gray blustery day had just gotten more depressing. When he turned around, Jackie was sitting in the chair Sperry had just vacated and was looking at her boss in a curious but knowing way.

"Tough one, huh."

"Yeah."

"Go about as you expected?"

"Pretty much."

"Anything a dirty rottin' old ship rat can do?"

Brendan laughed.

"I don't think so."

"Well, I'd better get back out there."

She scrunched up her nose, stuck out her tongue, and walked out.

A Long Farewell

The second semester had begun smoothly, and students and staff were nearing the end of the first full week of classes on Thursday, January 29, when Lena Davis ran up to Brendan, who was in the sophomore hallway during the break between second and third periods talking to Skip Daniels, one of the health and physical education teachers.

"Mr. Farrell, there's a fight upstairs!"

"Where, upstairs?"

"In the freshman hall."

Weaving through the crush of sophomores, Brendan escaped the congestion and sprinted up the east wing stairway, followed by Daniels. He could see the huddle of students as soon as he turned the corner from the staircase. Frank Blankenship was already on the scene, attending to Martin Bashore, whose nose and upper lip were bleeding profusely. Brendan pushed through the preponderance of freshmen students and confronted Blankenship.

"What happened?"

Blankenship turned to look at the tall student behind him, but before he could comment, Darrell Rhodes spoke.

"That little shit called me a sumbitch; that's what happened!"

"I did not," said the diminutive Bashore, who was holding a Kleenex to his nose. "I wasn't talking to you!"

"Yeah, well who was ya talkin' to, ya little shit?"

"I was just mad at my locker 'cause it wouldn't open."

Hearing enough, Brendan interrupted.

"Marty, what happened to your face?"

Fighting back tears in front of the students whom Blankenship and Daniels were dispersing, Bashore choked out that he had been struggling with his locker and called it a "sonofabitch." Suddenly, he was whirled around by his arm and punched in the face. Pointing with his right hand while holding his nose with his left, the shaken freshman said, "That guy did it!"

Brendan turned to Rhodes.

"Is that right?"

Not knowing how many others may have seen him, Rhodes made no attempt to deny it.

"Damn right, I did. And I'll do it again if he mouths off to me again like that."

Without turning his attention from Rhodes, Brendan said to his assistant principal, "Mr. Blankenship, please escort Mr. Rhodes to my office."

While Blankenship took Rhodes to the office, Brendan took Bashore to the clinic to have the school nurse, June Stellinger, attend to him. As June worked on Martin, Brendan called the boy's dad, thinking he could leave work more easily than the boy's mom who was a registered nurse in an intensive care unit. When Mr. Bashore arrived, Brendan explained what had happened and assured him that Darrell Rhodes would be dealt with severely. The father thanked Brendan for the call and concern, and left to take his son to the emergency room to get his nose examined. Brendan went immediately to the main office where he found Rhodes sitting sullenly on a bench and Frank talking quietly to Jackie.

"Mrs. Norris, please give Dr. Kline a call and tell him I'll have to postpone my meeting with him this morning. And tell him I'll bring him up to speed later today."

Brendan entered his office, and Darrell picked up some notebooks from the bench and followed him. Frank stopped at the outer office door.

"Mr. Farrell, will you need me for this?"

"No. Uh...well, if you have the time, Mr. Blankenship, maybe you could sit in."

"Sure."

Once the three sat down, Brendan did the talking.

"Darrell, I assume you remember what I told you before Christmas regarding any other assaults on students."

"No, what'd you..."

"So, what I'm gonna do is suspend you as of this moment

because your continued presence represents a threat to the safety of other students."

"That's bull..."

"Furthermore, I'm recommending to Dr. Kline that you be expelled for the remainder of the year. At this time, you may retrieve your belongings from your locker and return to the office immediately to sign the notice of the intent-to-suspend."

"And what if I don't leave?"

"I'll have the Maplemont police arrest you for trespassing on school grounds."

"Screw this. I'm leavin' now!"

"Suit yourself."

Once in the hallway and near the exit, Rhodes hollered, "Kiss my ass!"

Frank turned to Brendan.

"I don't think he likes you."

"Me? I thought he was talkin' to you."

"Not this time, Kemo Sabe."

As a courtesy, Brendan left a message for Mrs. Rhodes at the department store where she worked, and she returned his call about fifteen minutes later. He explained what had happened and the action he took and was planning to take. She said little during the call and asked only when the expulsion would take effect. Brendan said that if the superintendent accepted his recommendation, an expulsion hearing would probably occur sometime during the following week, depending on all the parties' schedules. The actual expulsion would commence immediately after the hearing. He told Donna Rhodes that he was dating the suspension for the next ten days in order to provide numerous options for the day of the meeting with Dr. Kline. He was taken aback by one of her few comments.

"I'll want my husband to be present for the expulsion hearing."

"I understand. Will he be available any time next week?"

"I don't know."

"Well, everything is subject to Dr. Kline's decision, of course."

"Yes. Well, goodbye then."

"I'll be in touch."

Brendan had left a message with Kline's secretary, and the superintendent returned his call shortly after lunch.

"Where's Rhodes now?"

"Probably at home. He drives to school."

"I believe he picks up his sister. Does his mother know of his suspension?"

"Yes. I spoke with her shortly after Darrell left. I told her my intention was to call her before he left, but he bolted out the door."

"How was she?"

"Frosty. She wants her husband to attend the expulsion hearing, if there is one."

"Wonderful!"

Brendan wasn't sure whether Kline would back him on the expulsion or not. Expulsions in Maplemont were as rare as pickup trucks, bad for the image. Besides, his current peace with the superintendent was tenuous at best, and Kline had no reason to put himself in peril with some loose cannon of a father just to save face for Brendan. In fact, he could very well look like a savior to the parents if he found some basis to reject or modify the principal's recommendation.

"Mrs. Rhodes is the custodial parent?"

"As far as I know."

"Well, it wouldn't do to bar the father from the meeting anyway. Giv'er a call and tell her we'll meet on Tuesday at four o'clock here at the board office. Between now and then, send me a narrative of the actions you and Frank have taken, attached to your recommendation for expulsion."

"What if the old man can't make it?"

"Tough."

A Long Farewell

"Uh, Jim."

"Yep."

"Thanks for your backing on this. I know it could be a donnybrook."

"That's why we make the big bucks. I'll be over Monday and we'll talk."

"See ya."

Brendan called Frank Blankenship and asked him to send him copies of all three of the Saturday School notifications so that he could make reference to dates and infractions in his memo to Kline. Fortunately, Frank had made the assignments as a substitute for suspensions and had used the appropriate notification forms.

On Monday, February 2, Kline arrived at Brendan's office shortly after morning announcements. He seemed uneasy when he gave Brendan the news.

"I just heard from Mrs. Rhodes, and she's asking for a postponement of the hearing."

"Why?"

"Says her husband can't be here tomorrow."

"What'd ya tell her?"

"I said I wanted to talk to you first, which I did."

Now Brendan was feeling uneasy.

"D'ya get my memo?"

"Yes, late Friday."

"Was there a problem with it?"

"No. It was very thorough. You and Frank have done a good job documenting your case."

"What, then?"

"Are you sure she has sole custody?"

"As a matter of fact, I just checked Darrell's records in the Guidance Office this morning, and the divorce decree says that she and the old man have joint custody of the kids."

"Well, that cuts it. I'm rescheduling for a week from tomorrow. She says her husband is not available at all this week, and I'll be in Columbus all day next Monday."

159

"Since Darrell's an emancipated eighteen-year-old, I don't think we're under any obligation to have either parent present, but I'm not absolutely sure."

"I'm not going to expel any student without a parent or parents present at the hearing if they want to be there."

"So be it. What time?"

"Eight o'clock. Let's get it over with."

At 7:45 a.m. on Tuesday, February 10, Brendan arrived at the board office, thinking he'd have a few minutes before Mr. and Mrs. Rhodes and their son Darrell arrived. He was wrong. As he came through the main door, he found them seated in the lobby: Bart Rhodes in a shirt and tie under a goose down jacket; Donna Rhodes in a long brown, wool coat with her ponderous purse on her lap; and Darrell Rhodes in a brown crewneck sweater, khaki cotton slacks, and blue nylon jacket.

"Good morning!" Brendan said cheerily, whistling through the graveyard at midnight. "Does Dr. Kline know you're here?"

"Yes," said Donna Rhodes as she glanced at her husband and son across from her.

"Well, we'll be right with you."

Brendan asked the receptionist if Kline was in, and she told him he was to go right on back. When he entered Kline's office, Brendan found him standing behind his desk reading from some papers. Without looking up he said, "Are you ready for this?"

"I dunno. That's a pretty hostile group out there."

"Yes. Well, some fights you can pick and some you can't."

"I believe that's the first time I've ever seen Darrell in anything but fatigues."

"Go get 'em."

Brendan went to the lobby and asked the Rhodes family to join him in the superintendent's office.

Donna Rhodes was about 5'5" tall and a little overweight.

A Long Farewell

Her graying hair and troubled countenance suggested a woman of 50 or 60. She probably wasn't a day over 42 or 43. Bart Rhodes had a full head of straight, dark brown hair that seemed to have been combed flat while still wet that morning. He was right at six feet, a little pot-bellied but slender in appearance. He was about 45 but looked considerably younger than his wife whose premature aging was probably in no small part his responsibility. As the parents and son seated themselves in chairs arranged in front of Kline's desk, Brendan took a chair off to their right. Kline introduced himself, and then began his preamble without any small talk.

"Darrell, you and your parents know, of course, the purpose of this hearing. I have a written recommendation before me from Mr. Farrell, who is urging me on the basis of your disciplinary history to expel you from Maplemont High School for the remainder of the school year. He specifically states your assault on Martin Bashore as the defining behavior that justifies your expulsion. You now have an opportunity to speak on your own behalf as to why I should not proceed as Mr. Farrell recommends."

Brendan couldn't help but note Kline's repeated emphasis upon his principal's recommendation to expel, which, obviously, it was, but he wondered if Kline wasn't playing Pontius Pilate.

"I have somethin' ta say here, before ya go any further."

Bart Rhodes jumped into the fray early.

"Farrell and that assistant principal Blankenship been after my boy since he got here. They never care what them other boys done to Darrell. They jist figure he's bigger, so he's guilty."

"Yeah, they don't even let me talk."

"That's pretty piss-poor, I'd say. Not to give a boy his chance. He's got rights too."

"Mr. Rhodes, this very hearing is held to protect your son's rights, but based on the documents before me, Mr. Farrell and Mr. Blankenship appear to have given Darrell

161

every opportunity to correct his behavior and every notice of his ultimate consequence."

"The only opportunity that principal ever gave me was a suspension and now this expulsion!"

"Darrell, the suspension I gave you followed three Saturday School assignments, each of which was an option to a suspension."

Bart Rhodes tried to speak again, but Kline cut him off.

"Regardless of your opinion of Mr. Farrell's or Mr. Blankenship's actions, Darrell and Mr. and Mrs. Rhodes, what must be determined this morning is whether what Mr. Farrell has stated as the basis of his recommendation is accurate and whether I should act on his recommendation."

"What's he sayin' 'bout Darrell?"

"What he's saying is that after three previous Saturday School assignments given to Darrell by Mr. Blankenship for your son's physical intimidation of other students, all under-classmen, he, Mr. Farrell, suspended Darrell for three days for a physical assault on freshman Mitchell Shapiro. Mr. Farrell further states that at the time of Darrell's suspension, he was warned that a future, similar infraction would result in a recommendation for an expulsion. Having struck fresh-man Martin Bashore in the face on January 29 and sent him to the emergency room, Darrell is now being recommended for an expulsion for the rest of the year. Is all of this cor-rect?"

"How come he suspended Darrell if he wanted him expelled?"

"I asked if what I said is correct."

At first, no one said anything. Then Donna Rhodes spoke for the first time.

"Mr. Kline, if you expel Darrell from Maplemont, can he go to another school this year?"

"By law, not to another public school in the State of Ohio. And the parochial and private schools have been wary of tak-ing expelled students of late."

A Long Farewell

"So you're saying that if you agree to Mr. Farrell's recommendation, Darrell will lose a whole school year?"

"Depending upon his mid-year grades, yes."

"He'll be 19 in April. He'll never go back to school."

Bart Rhodes came to life and addressed Brendan directly. "Think about that, mister. You're ruinin' this kid's life over a damned little punch inna nose."

Darrell's grin in response to his father's trivialization of the attack did not escape the notice of Brendan and Kline.

"Whether Mr. Farrell's recommendation ruins Darrell's life is up to Darrell, Mr. and Mrs. Rhodes, but I have yet to hear whether you dispute the principal's account of the facts. Darrell, are there any inaccuracies here?"

"I couldn't tell ya."

"In that case I have no reason to reject Mr. Farrell's recommendation for expulsion. Please be notified that Darrell is hereby expelled from Maplemont High School for the remainder of the school year. The terms of his removal from Maplemont will be included in the notice of expulsion that my secretary will send to you in this morning's mail. Shall I have her send all copies to your address, Mrs. Rhodes?"

"Bart?"

"Yeah, send 'em there."

Still seated and clutching her purse as the four men rose, Donna Rhodes said while looking through the bay window behind Kline's desk, "May I come in later and pick up copies of Darrell's records?"

Brendan answered.

"Yes, you may, Mrs. Rhodes, but you might want to give the Guidance Office a call first to avoid a bit of a wait."

"I understand."

"Darrell," Brendan said, "you understand that you cannot be on school grounds during this expulsion?"

Darrell shot a portentous look at Brendan that said much more than his surly response.

"I know what I can do and what I can't."

Pausing in the doorway of Kline's office, Bart Rhodes underscored Darrell's threatening look and tone, spewing, "Your time's comin', mister!"

Brendan returned to his office around 9:00 a.m. after discussing the hearing with Kline, who seemed very detached. Through the day Brendan was struck several times by Darrell Rhodes's ominous bearing and Bart Rhodes's parting comment. About 4:30, he rose from his desk chair, put on his suit coat, and gazed out upon the relentless gloom of another winter day in Ohio. Even though others were unaware, Brendan knew that he would soon tender his resignation and then retire at the end of the school year, his thirtieth in public education.

***

At its February meeting, the Maplemont Board of Education approved by a 5-0 vote the superintendent's recommendation to adopt a course of study for an advanced placement chemistry program for upper classmen. Unlike some proposals that were vigorously argued in executive session, the A. P. Chemistry sailed through closed-session discussions with only one proviso by three members: John Sperry was not to teach the course. Furthermore, Dr. James Kline was strongly urged to have Sperry reassigned to science courses less critical to the success of applications to prestigious colleges and universities. Since Kline was due for contract renewal, he got the message, and as a consequence, so did Brendan Farrell.

On Monday, March 16, Brendan put a message in John Sperry's mailbox before the chemistry teacher arrived, asking him to meet in Brendan's office during sixth period. When Jackie called Brendan later that day to advise him of Sperry's arrival, her principal was uncharacteristically professional.

"Thanks, Jackie. Please tell John I'll see him in a moment."

Staring for a few minutes at the earlier budding trees, on which the branches were dancing in the wind outside his window, he decided to call Jackie back.

"Yes?"

"Any chance a your sittin' on Sperry's lap out there while you stroke 'is thigh and tell 'im his ass ain't teachin' chemistry next year?"

For the first time during her employment at Maplemont, Norris nearly lost her composure, not from the measure of Brendan's impropriety but by the image it conjured.

"I...I don't think there's any chance of that...no."

"Then let the games begin."

Brendan walked over and opened his door, and Sperry took his seat abruptly.

"John, I've now conducted two formal observations of your classes during the second semester, and I've completed your final evaluation for the year. In it, I've stated that I'll be reassigning you to a physical and environmental science schedule next year. Although our meeting today wasn't scheduled as an evaluation meeting, I wanted to tell you in advance part of what the evaluation will contain. At your choosing, we can conduct the evaluation meeting at this time, and I can let you read the written statement now."

"What would be the point of delaying it?"

"Only to give you advance notice of the intent of an evaluation meeting."

"Why didn't you?"

"As I said, I wanted to let you know something of the substance of my remarks before we sat down formally. I'm not saying that we can't or shouldn't conduct the meeting at a future day with greater notice. I'm simply saying that if you prefer, we can conduct the meeting at this time, and I'll hand you my written statement."

"I see no point in waiting."

"I caution you that you may want to talk to a building rep before you do."

"You're not firing me, are you?"

"Of course not."

"Is the evaluation damaging?"

"Not at all. Unless you perceive reassignment as damaging."

"I do. But I know you have the right to reassign me. I've already discussed that with Martin."

Martin Salsbury was the Maplemont Teachers Association president who could dig his heels in when he had the traction, but he was realistic in choosing his fights.

"Does that mean you wish to wait or read the evaluation at this time?"

"Let's do it."

Brendan handed John the carefully worded evaluation that unintentionally damned the teacher by a faint praise that provided reasonable basis for reassignment because of the teacher's "strengths in working with less motivated science students."

John sped through the document and set it down in front of himself.

"May I use your pen?"

Handing John the pen, Brendan's fears were apparently confirmed: in spite his best efforts to the contrary, his relationship with this teacher had become adversarial, and he had lost a friend in the workplace.

"Hold on a second, and I'll make you a copy, John."

"Just put it in my mailbox. Thanks."

John walked out, and Brendan had that old feeling again. Grace Miller would reappear like Marley's ghost every time a John Sperry situation arose. He knew he was only the point man in an action unequivocally sought by three members of the board. Even so, Kline had been quite clear with his principal that no reference to board disposition should be made in Brendan's written evaluation. But Brendan couldn't help hearing that soulful voice of a young band instructor who had relied upon him so long ago: "I thought you were different; I thought I could count on you."

The next day, Tuesday, March 17, Brendan arrayed him-self in his clownish green suspenders, green and white striped shirt, and blue tie with green shamrocks and headed to work to face the abuse and guffaws he would take from his staff, particularly Bensman, who always swore he'd wear his King Willy black bowler and orange sash but didn't. Under his blue suit coat the effect was pretty much obscured if he had to assume some dignity in haste, but when Brendan shucked the coat, he looked as mad as a March hare. The March Madness of college basketball was now under way, and most of the male staff and many of the female staff mem-bers were checking their bracket sheets carefully each morn-ing to determine their status in the annual pool. Brendan walked into the teachers' workroom around 7:30 to shoot the breeze with the early morning gang and take his first assaults of the day on his sartorial accomplishments.

Brendan received the expected boo-hiss from Bensman and various cracks from Foxworth, who likened him to a cross between the foppish Osrick from *Hamlet* and the drunken jester from *The Wizard of Id*. Shortly after Brendan grabbed his orange juice, Joe Russo walked in with his copy of *The Wall Street Journal* and gave Brendan a phony double take that said as much nonverbally as Bensman and Foxworth had said orally. The taciturn Russo was easily the most erudite teacher on the staff, and he could be typically found toting some scholarly periodical or monograph to remain abreast of current events or historical perspectives. Joe taught the senior, government classes, but he was per-fectly at ease teaching history or economics. Russo rarely spoke, but when he did, Brendan listened.

That afternoon the revelers on the Maplemont staff beat a path to Finnegan's to get the beer flowing early. The next day was a teaching day, so what they'd lose in time at the bar, they'd make up in consumption. By the time Brendan arrived, the bar was rife with laughter and vibrating with

167

loud banter and blaring Irish music that added nothing but noise. The traditional pitchers of green beer were tipping, and along with a hug from Kathy Linn, a Spanish teacher, he was given a clear plastic cup of food-colored draught beer that he nearly drained in two gulps. Most of his crew were either seated at or gathered around three or four tables in a corner. Foxworth fired the first salvo.

"Don't try to tell us you've been workin' 'til now."

"Get behind me, Satan!"

"Satan, hell. He wouldn't waste his time here. He's already got this bunch stamped for delivery."

Damn, Brendan thought, *I'm going to miss these guys.*

***

By April, Brendan was nearly finished with the master schedule, and, working from the conflict matrix, he was running algorithms that were producing a good distribution of students in just about all sections. Most, if not all, of Brendan's success each year with the master schedule derived from the analytic and foresighted thinking of Dave Schafer, one of Maplemont's three guidance counselors.

Schafer was the gregarious and unofficial public relations man for Maplemont High School, and while his worth to the school in general and Brendan in particular was inestimable, he never missed an opportunity to parlay his contributions into a budget bump for a conference in someplace like San Francisco, New Orleans, Denver, Miami, or Chicago. Curiously, those conferences in the Sun Belt almost always occurred in January, February, or March. Dave would raise his budget request just as he was sitting down with Brendan to discuss the master schedule. When he had come into the office in March with his yellow tablet in hand, Brendan knew what was coming.

"Brendan, you have a minute to look at some preliminary suggestions for the master schedule?"

A Long Farewell

"I've been waitin' on ya, David. Where've ya been?"

"Well, actually, with the new A. P. Chemistry sections, I've hadta spend a lot more time on potential problems this year."

And, Brendan thought, *you want to spend a lot more money on potential travel next year.*

"Dave, for once, let's just start with how much your suggestions are gonna cost me."

Schafer flashed a smile that would have done a Cheshire cat proud. Brendan wondered absurdly if one day only the smile would come through the door.

"Why, Brendan, you hurt my feelings."

"Why, David, I couldn't hurt your feelings with a nine-pound hammer."

"Well, there is a conference on distance learning that as a counselor at a school like Maplemont I really should attend."

"When is it?"

"Next February."

"Where is it?"

"Uh...Orlando."

"And you'd rather not have to go?"

"Really."

In his best falsetto voice, Brendan went into his best Brer Rabbit.

" 'O please, Brer Fox, don't fling me in dat brier patch!' "

"What?"

" 'You kin roas me, hang me, drown me, er skin me, Brer Fox, but do fer de Lord's sake don't fling me in dat brier-patch!' "

Brendan loved Uncle Remus stories and regarded Joel Chandler Harris as the definitive local color writer.

"I dunno what the hell you're talkin' about."

"That's 'cause you're an illiterate, self-serving swine."

"I resemble that remark!"

"Now, how much is this gonna cost me?"

169

"With my flight, lodging, meals, and registration, about fifteen hundred and some change."

"You understand that's your total guidance budget for the year."

"Now, wait a minute. I've got C.A.T.'s to order and tons of other materials and supplies."

"You should've been a wiseguy, ya know that."

"I'm good with concrete."

"Wuddya have for me?"

The last two months of any school year were always tense for a high school principal; everything seemed to happen at once. Particularly unnerving to Brendan was knowing that almost invariably at least one student would have his or her name misspelled on an award or mispronounced at a banquet or assembly, not to mention the occasional student who was omitted entirely. In such a case, Brendan became anathema in Maplemont, where parent tolerance of administrative error was only slightly greater than being seen by a friend, or worse yet, an enemy, at K-Mart. If one Maplemonter did see another in pursuit of a blue-light special, each was like the turd in the punch bowl, observed but not acknowledged.

As Brendan prepared for his imminent retirement, he decided to tell no one in the Maplemont City Schools of his plan. His hope was to delay the announcement as long as possible and avoid a lame-duck status and the staff suspicion that he was just coasting. It also allowed him to leave quickly and without any spurious celebrations. When he walked out the door at the end of June, he'd be gone for good.

***

The dresser drawer slid open easily and quietly and presented the socks and underwear that concealed what lay beneath them. When the soft-cloth drawstring bag was withdrawn from the drawer and opened, it revealed the elegance

of its contents. The replica of the 1911 production .45 caliber combat pistol gleamed, even in the dimly lighted room.
The bead-blasted steel frame and slide and the double-dia-
mond rosewood grips made for a thing of beauty even an
ardent opponent of handguns could admire. With its five-
inch barrel and eight-round magazine, the semi-automatic's
33-ounce weight provided its handler with a feeling of reassuring heft and a sense of plenary power. But this gun was
no museum piece to be kept under glass and admired; it was
a deadly efficient, sanguinary apparatus that could deliver a
four-inch shot group at forty yards and dispatch quarry with
an awesome finality.

***

The month of May at Maplemont was a white-knuckled
time for Brendan and other school personnel, but by the first
week of June, the school had processed through its crucible
of a National Honor Society induction, a performance of *The
Music Man*, the awards assembly, the baccalaureate service,
and the spring sports banquets. Even the senior prank, a
condom stretched over every classroom and office door handle in the building, caused no serious disruption of classes.
Monday, June 3 was the first day of examinations for freshmen, sophomores, and juniors, and that evening the seniors
would receive their last hurrahs from families, faculty, and
friends.

With the remaining students arriving and departing on a
staggered schedule, Brendan didn't come in to the office
Monday morning until 9:00, knowing that he probably
wouldn't leave until well after 10:00 p.m. As he sailed
through the office door, Jackie was taking yet another call
from a parent asking for a deferment for a son or daughter's
exam. She hung up, wrote herself a note, and waited for the
next call.

"Morning!"

John Hagan

"Hi. Sorry I'm so late. Been deluged?"

"Little bit."

"Well, I'm gonna head in here for a few minutes to go over my checklist for tonight while I'm still thinking about it."

"Okay, but I think everything's ready."

Her remark was an understatement. The only checklist of any importance was hers, and Brendan knew she'd have everything planned by the numbers. All he had to do was show up and not screw it up. Sometimes he wondered if he was even necessary. Good secretaries could run any school he'd ever been in, and administrators with half a brain knew it.

That night, graduation couldn't have gone more smoothly, largely owing to Jackie's planning. Maplemont's stately auditorium, distinguished by its ornate proscenium arch, served once again to bring elegance and grandeur to the proceedings. Built on the school grounds in the 1920's to accommodate both school and community functions, it blended harmoniously with the other buildings. At 7:00 p.m., Brendan Farrell welcomed relatives, friends, and teachers to the Maplemont High School commencement ceremony.

***

The eight .45 caliber hollow points lay on the kitchen table. One-by-one they were inserted into the spring-loaded magazine. The full metal jacket was pushed into the handle and popped into place. The steel slide was drawn back and released. Fully stocked and activated, the 1911 exuded power, the power to correct wrongs, to set things right.

***

As Brendan drove to his last administrative meeting of the year on June 6, he kept handling the envelopes that lay on the seat next to him. They contained his resignation letter

172

addressed to Dr. James Kline and a copy for Carl Ritchie, Treasurer of Maplemont City Schools. Before arriving at the meeting, Brendan went to the board office and asked the receptionist to place the letters on the superintendent's and treasurer's desks.

Since the June meeting was the last until August, it was traditionally held at a restaurant, and it usually amounted to turning in final reports and little else but lunch and casual talk. Owing to his side trip to the board office, Brendan was the last to arrive, and the others were already seated at one of the long tables on the open-air porch. The meeting, such as it was, began immediately after Brendan sat down, and after some brief discussion of budgets and funding for the next year, Kline waxed eloquent on district successes for the past year. Brendan had advised Kline in advance that he was holding his last staff meeting of the year at 1:00 p.m. and would have to leave early.

When Brendan arrived at the high school, the counter in the main office was covered with open cartons, each serving as a receptacle for the specific forms and records that teachers deposited as part of the checkout procedure. By 12:15, most of the teachers were finished, and the few who weren't were making hasty trips back to their classrooms to find forms or records they'd forgotten. Brendan went on back to his office to rehearse what he'd say to his staff. At 12:55, he walked out of his office, heading for the library, the unofficial high school meeting place.

"Any words of encouragement?"

"Good luck."

Jackie had not looked up. She knew what he was about to tell his staff, and she didn't want him to see the tears.

Brendan warmed up with some rather mundane end-of-the-year reminders that he could easily have put in a memo. Pausing to gather himself, he faltered twice before stammering out his poignant announcement that some took initially as a jest. He had hoped for something profound, but what he expressed was a hackneyed statement of his gratitude to the staff that sounded like a dumb jock's post-game checklist of clichés. He exited the library immediately after his farewell and repaired to the service staff lounge to compose himself. The only measure of comfort he took from his clumsy good-bye was that his teachers had heard of his resignation before anyone else but Jackie and that they had heard it from him. When he returned to his office over an hour later, he closed the door and brooded for the rest of the day.

At 4:20 p.m., Jackie tapped on Brendan's door and then opened it slowly.

"I've pretty much gone as far as I can today. Three or four are coming back tomorrow to finish up."

"That's fine. Get goin'."

"I'll talk to you tomorrow."

"Okay. Uh...what time are you going to lunch tomorrow?"

"I don't know. I haven't thought about it. The secretaries will probably get together. Why?"

"I don't care when you leave, but could you be back by one?"

"Oh yeah. I have too much to do to be gone for very long. I'll be back by then."

"Ordinarily I wouldn't care but I..."

"I'll be back."

"It's just that I..."

"You don't have to explain. I'll be back."

She withdrew from the doorway and went to her desk for her purse. Brendan got up and replaced her in the doorway.

"Jackie, I hope..."

She turned and faced him.

For the first time since he had known her, Brendan noticed that the seemingly insurmountable Norris composure was in peril; her face was red. Turning, she walked out.

Brendan's appointment at the A Site to scan his grade sheets was at 10:00 a.m. on Friday, so arriving at the office at 9:00, he had little time before leaving again. Jackie was as busy as usual, taking calls and finishing the storage and dispatching of forms.

"Well, I'm gonna run these down to scan. How many are left to check out?"

"Just John Sperry. He said he had more to do since his room is changing."

"When's he checkin' out?"

"He asked if he could have until early this afternoon, and that's okay because I won't be finished yet anyway."

"When are you goin' to lunch?"

"I'm going to meet some of the other secretaries at the Cracker Barrel at 11:45, but I'll be back by one."

"Don't hurry. If you're not back by one, it's no big deal."

"I'll be back."

She turned and looked out the window, and Brendan knew that further discussion would be disastrous.

By the time he scanned his grades, Brendan was pushing 11:30. Returning to his office at 11:50, he dropped the stack of grade sheets on his desk and headed into the halls. He stuck his head into the weight room and was greeted by the moldy smell of indoor-outdoor carpeting. The secretaries had gone to lunch, and the maintenance guys were outdoors working on the grounds. He walked in and sat on one of the weight benches. He was well into some pensive wool-gathering when a voice at the door startled him.

"Hey, Bubba, you really surprised the hell out of us yesterday."

It was Dave Schafer.

"Pleasantly, I hope."

"You know better than that."

"I really pissed down my leg, didn't I."

"We struggled with you."

"Damn, I was embarrassed afterwards!"

"Embarrassed. Why?"

"I must've looked like the village idiot."

"You looked like someone who cared about leavin' us."

Schafer sat down and, in a way only he could, he engaged Brendan in a cathartic conversation for the next hour and lifted his principal's spirits for the first time in weeks.

"Oh shit! It's almost one o'clock."

"And?"

"I've gotta get back to my office."

"I'll walk down with you. I need to check my mailbox."

Brendan and Dave drifted out of the weight room and down the hall past the chemistry and physics labs. They were about to turn the corner into the hallway leading to the main office when a voice behind them hailed Brendan.

"Mr. Farrell, wait up."

Brendan and Dave turned and saw John Sperry approaching them. When the chemistry teacher reached them at the junction of the two halls, Brendan could read the choler in his demeanor.

"I have some keys for ya."

As Brendan reached for the keys, he was only peripherally aware of the person approaching him from the direction of the main office.

The .45 came up to eye level and discharged two slugs in measured succession. The first pierced Brendan's left lung and broke his third rib before exiting his back and knocking him against the wall. The second hit him just below his clavicle and severed his trachea before embedding itself in the wall.

"Oh, my God!" yelled Schafer.

"Oh, my God!" gasped Sperry.

Brendan slumped to the floor and stared up as Schafer and Sperry crouched beside him, stunned.

O my God, prayed Brendan, *I am heartily sorry for...*

As he looked up through the fading light, Brendan did not see the benevolent eyes of God the Father; he saw only the dispassionate eyes of Gregor the insect, whose body was spattered with blood and cratered in two places. Brendan slipped first into unconsciousness and then into oblivion.

A Long Farewell

At 1:05, an attractive woman got out of a blue sedan in the parking lot near the stadium and headed up the walkway to Maplemont High School. As she did, she watched a matronly woman exit the door and place something in a large brown purse. Passing one another, the arriving woman spoke first.

"Good afternoon," said Jackie Norris, affably.

"Good afternoon," said Donna Rhodes, heedlessly.

About an hour after the shooting, Donna Rhodes was in handcuffs being guided by Maplemont police toward the back seat of a cruiser in front of her house. Addressing the crowd of onlookers at the curb across the street, she offered her apologia.

"He ruined my boy's life!"

`Macbeth`—William Shakespeare

Author

John Hagan was born in Presque Isle, Maine, and shortly thereafter his family returned to Dayton, Ohio, where he was reared. A career educator and ancestrally Irish, he believes the Celtic influence in American classrooms often effectuates the comical, the poignant, and the sublime. While teachers are sometimes perceived as a bit stodgy and bland, John regards them as the intriguing equal of lawyers, police, doctors, and other professionals often rendered in fiction. Imbued with a profound love of the land, he inclines toward country settings.

A retired secondary school English teacher and administrator, John was also an adjunct, composition instructor at The University of Dayton, where his students' essays often provided his clearest understanding of current thinking among young adults.

John divides much of his time between his home in Springboro, Ohio and his labor of love, a forty-acre farm in Highland County, Ohio. His many days spent "down on the farm" have yielded a consummate respect for the people who preserve and protect the land. He has written *A Long Farewell* as an energizing experience that draws upon enduring personal interests. John earned undergraduate and graduate degrees in English and secondary school administration at Thomas More College, Xavier University, and Miami University.

www.ingramcontent.com/pod-product-compliance
Lightning Source LLC
Chambersburg PA
CBHW020519120726
47904CB00003B/895